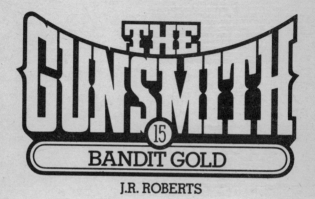

THE GUNSMITH

15

BANDIT GOLD

J.R. ROBERTS

CHARTER BOOKS, NEW YORK

All characters in this book are fictitious.
Any resemblance to actual persons, living or dead,
is purely coincidental.

THE GUNSMITH #15: BANDIT GOLD
A Charter Book/published by arrangement with the author

PRINTING HISTORY
Ace edition/April 1983

ISBN: 0-441-30872-4

Charter Books are published by Charter Communications, Inc.
200 Madison Avenue, New York, N.Y. 10016.
PRINTED IN THE UNITED STATES OF AMERICA

Dedicated to
Ms. Damaris Rowland

Best Wishes
Always

THE GUNSMITH #15
BANDIT GOLD

ONE

Hell is supposed to be the final destination of evil souls after death, but many citizens of Brownsville, Texas would have claimed that it had arrived in their town that summer. The afternoon heat created an inferno for the living—be they pure of heart or devoted sinner.

Neither description aptly fit Clint Adams, but he had ridden into the furnace and had to suffer along with everybody else. Clint shifted his backside along the wooden seat of the wagon, feeling the sweat-soaked cloth cling to his buttocks. He held the reins loosely in one hand and used the other to dab his face and neck with a wetted-down neckerchief, allowing the team to set their own leisurely pace. Occasionally he'd glance back to see how Duke was holding up. The big black Arabian gelding, tied to the rear of the wagon, trotted along without any sign of fatigue. Still, white lather streaked the animal's magnificent coat, evidence that he too needed to get out of the heat of the merciless Texas sun.

"No more poker," Clint vowed hoarsely, although he knew he'd never keep that promise.

Well, it would be a while before he got into another high-stakes game with a tableful of players he didn't know. He'd sat down to a card game of five-card stud in a saloon in Laredo and started off pretty well, winning enough hands to get overconfident. He broke two of his normally ironclad rules: He'd allowed himself to drink too much free liquor and paid too much attention to a stunning redhead who hovered by his side throughout the game.

He'd gotten a bit careless and wound up losing enough of his bankroll to put himself in a bind. Well, that sort of thing happened from time to time. The old proverb about being unlucky at cards, however, held true after the game. The redhead and Clint spent an enjoyable night together before he left Laredo.

Brownsville was a hell of a distance from Laredo, but it was still the closest honest-to-God city. That's what Clint needed right now, a city full of people. Lots of people meant plenty of potential customers. One nice thing about Texas was that just about everybody owned a gun and most folks owned quite a few. That meant there'd be lots of firearms in need of parts, repairs or modifications. What better place for the "Gunsmith" to practice his trade?

Clint sighed, thinking of the irony involved in how he'd gotten that title. He hadn't been a real gunsmith when a newspaperman discovered that Deputy Sheriff Clint Adams, who had already acquired an unwanted reputation as being one of the fastest guns in the West, had an expertise for fixing and modifying firearms. Wishing to add color to his story, the newsman christened him the "Gunsmith" and he'd been trying to cope with the moniker ever since. He never tried to live up to it and he'd often tried to live it down, but he'd eventually decided he simply had to live with it.

Brownsville had grown rapidly since the War Between the States to become one of the key cities in Texas. There were several large cattle ranches in the area and drives of white-faced Herefords from Baltimore were delivered to Corpus Christi and eventually found their way to Brownsville, making it the livestock capital of the Lone Star State.

Saloons, tanneries, blacksmith shops and even haberdasheries made a good profit in Brownsville. It was located close enough to the border to attract business from Mexican cattle buyers and close enough to the Gulf to attract a lot of seaport trade, and with the addition of the railroad, business coming in and going out of the city had increased as well.

The streets of Brownsville were flanked by an assortment of buildings, some of them four stories high. However, the severe heat had driven most of the citizens indoors. To Clint, Brownsville seemed to be the biggest ghost town in the world. An old man in a rocking chair sat on a plankwalk, apparently napping—if he hadn't suffered from sunstroke. The only other living creatures in Clint's view were four men on horseback, approaching from the opposite end of town.

Clint's wagon rolled past a brick bank with bars in its windows and moved on to one of the local saloons. He noticed some slight movement beyond the batwings and a soft whistle drew his attention to an open window at the floor above. A young, painted-faced whore smiled down at him.

"Afternoon, ma'am," Clint greeted with a polite tip of his low-crowned stetson.

Actually, the only commodity offered in the saloon that appealed to Clint was a couple of beers to wash out the trail dust. He glanced at the sheriff's office on the opposite side of the street and debated giving it a visit first.

No real reason to. It was just a habit of courtesy he'd developed over the years to let the local law know he was in town. The beers seemed like a better idea, due to his hard-earned thirst, but first he'd have to take care of Duke and his rig.

Clint spotted a livery stable and headed toward it. The four men on horseback drew closer. They were a scruffy-looking group, covered with dust and smeared by sweat and dirt. The horsemen gazed intently at the Gunsmith as though expecting trouble from him, but Clint merely nodded. His expression didn't reveal the fact that he'd recognized a familiar face among the group. A face he'd seen on wanted posters in three states.

"How do you fellers like Brownsville so far?" a beefy, red-faced horseman inquired, tugging at the brim of his Montana peak hat.

"What I'd like is some goddamn beer, Clem," a lanky fellow with large tobacco-stained teeth answered.

Clem Burns, the Gunsmith thought, his suspicions now confirmed. Burns was a bank robber who didn't mind killing anyone who got in his way. Clint glanced over the faces of the other three horsemen. Besides the lanky character with the ugly teeth, there was a bearded, bearlike man who didn't appear to be too familiar with soap and water, and a towheaded youngster with blond peach fuzz on his cheeks. The kid had big, innocent blue eyes, which the Gunsmith realized probably concealed the soul of a cold-blooded killer.

"Yeah, Clem," the bearded man complained. "It's hot enough to fry a horntoad. Let's get a beer afore we get on with the job."

"Reckon we got time for a brew," Burns answered. He sounded like a bullfrog with an Alabama accent.

Clint didn't let the men know he'd paid any attention to their conversation. He calmly steered his rig to the livery stable. An old man emerged from the building, dressed in a pair of overalls and a long-john shirt with big wet stains under both arms.

"Howdy, son," the liveryman greeted him with a toothless smile.

Clint said howdy back and turned over his rig and horses to the old-timer. "Take extra care to see that my gear on the wagon isn't disturbed, and I want you to treat that big black gelding to the best you've got. All right?"

"Sure, son," the old man nodded eagerly when Clint handed him a five dollar bill.

"I'll be back in a little while to give you a hand and check on my belongings," Clint added. "Right now, I have to see the sheriff."

"The sheriff?" the old-timer frowned. "Somethin' wrong, young feller?"

"Not yet," the Gunsmith replied as he headed for the lawman's office.

TWO

Sheriff Matt Wilson looked up from his desk when he heard the door open. His great red walrus mustache accented his frown when he saw the tall, slim stranger. Clint's dust-laced denim didn't disturb him, nor did he jump to any conclusions about the scar that marked the Gunsmith's otherwise pleasant features. Wilson's reaction was based on the gunbelt strapped around Clint's lean waist. The holster was strapped low on his right thigh and the metal of the Colt revolver encased in it was obviously clean and freshly oiled.

The Gunsmith recognized the lawman's reaction and realized Wilson had mistaken him for a gunfighter. He offered a smile and extended his hand as he approached the desk.

"Sheriff, my name is Clint Adams," he began.

Wilson's eyes expanded in their sockets. "Do tell?" he eagerly took Clint's hand and shook it. "You're the Gunsmith?"

"Some people call me that," Clint admitted.

"I've heard that whenever you come to a place you check in with the law and let 'em know about it," the sheriff grinned, obviously pleased to meet someone he'd clearly admired for years. "I know you get into trouble from time to time, but way I hear it is you never start none, so you're welcome to stay here in Brownsville as long as you like."

6

"I appreciate that, Sheriff," Clint nodded. "But I think you ought to know something."

Wilson's smile fell. "What's that?"

"I think there's a pretty good chance there's going to be an attempt to rob your bank."

"Sweet Jesus," Wilson whispered. "You sure?"

"I just saw Clem Burns and three other hardcases head over to the saloon. They were talking about having a beer before the 'job' and Burn's profession is robbing banks."

"Shit!" the sheriff groaned. "My deputies are clean on the other side of town makin' their rounds!"

The Gunsmith had already moved to the window and watched as the blond kid and the bearded man emerged from the saloon. The pair took three horses by the reins and led the animals into an alley situated between the saloon and a tannery. Wilson joined Clint at the window.

"That's two of them," the Gunsmith told him.

"Well, they ain't headin' toward the bank," Wilson remarked. "Could be you've made a mistake, friend."

Clint shook his head. "That alley leads behind the saloon and that means they can just move over to the rear of the bank. Think of it this way, Sheriff—this office is right across the street from the bank. If you looked out and saw four horses hitched in front of it, you'd be apt to suspect there might be a robbery in progress. If there's only one horse, well, how many men would be bold enough to try to hold up a bank alone? So those two took the horses around back, out of view, but close enough to come to the aid of their partners if any shooting starts."

"By God," the sheriff whispered. "Reckon you got a point, Adams."

"Call me Clint."

"Sure, Clint," Wilson agreed. "How do you figure we should handle this?"

"Well, it's your town, Sheriff," Clint began. "But might I suggest that you get a rifle, an accurate one that you're familiar with, and station yourself here at the door of this office and cover me."

"What are you going to do?" the sheriff asked.

"I'll head over to the saloon and then move around to the back of the bank and see if I can get the drop on those two. If they'll surrender, then maybe we can catch Burns in the act and take care of this business without any call for gunplay. How's that sound?"

"Er . . . well. . . ." Wilson shrugged. "Just fine. . . ."

The Gunsmith opened the door and left the sheriff's office, hoping the lawman would prove to be more competent with a rifle than he seemed to be with strategy. Clint strolled to the saloon without glancing toward the bank or back at the sheriff's office. As Clint was about to enter the saloon, the batwings parted and Clem Burns, carrying a saddlebag over his shoulder, stepped onto the plankwalk, followed by the lanky outlaw, nearly brushing into the Gunsmith. Burns hurried to the hitching-rail and untied the reins of a big sorrel stallion.

Clint barely gave the men a second glance as he pushed through the batwings and strode into the barroom. The saloon was larger than most, with a number of card tables, chairs and a typical sawdust floor. Clint noticed a piano in one corner, but the handful of weary customers didn't merit the efforts of the player, a heavy-set black man who sat at his bench sipping beer. There was also a small roulette table.

In the evenings, the saloon probably had some pretty interesting games of chance to choose from, Clint guessed. It was too bad he'd sworn off gambling—for a while. Maybe if he got a large enough bankroll built up, he'd give the place a try. The Gunsmith walked to the long, leather-topped bar.

"What'll it be?" a stocky man with a craggy face, stationed behind the counter inquired. His attitude seemed to suggest he would have preferred not to be disturbed with customers. *Maybe someone else works nights*, Clint thought, hoping so for the sake of the saloon's business.

"Would you show me where the back or side door to this place is, friend?" the Gunsmith replied.

"What?" the bartender's eyes narrowed. "You just come in here, mister!"

Clint nodded. "And I hope to come back soon and enjoy a beer or two and some more of your sparkling company, but right now I'd like to know where that other door is."

"Get out the way you came."

"The sheriff sent me," Clint said sharply. "Now, unless you don't have any money in the bank next door, you'd better show me where that door is before the four men who just left this place rob it."

"Uh,"—the bartender swallowed hard—"it's over that way."

The Gunsmith followed the man's pointing finger and found the side door. He opened it and stepped into an alley located between the saloon and the bank. Staying close to the brick wall of the latter, Clint moved to the rear of the building and eased his Colt from its holster.

The revolver wasn't exactly a Colt anymore. Clint had modified it, altering the frame and the cylinder, the trigger mechanism and the hammer bar, until he'd converted the single-action model to fire double-action so that it didn't have to be cocked between shots and could thus be fired more rapidly.

With his converted Colt in hand, Clint peeked around

the corner of the bank and saw the bearded outlaw and
the blond kid with the three horses they'd escorted into
the other alley a few minutes before. The older man
held the reins to the animals while his young partner
drew a Winchester carbine from a saddle boot and
worked the lever to jack a shell into the chamber.

"Figure there'll be shootin', Moe?" the kid asked, his
grin suggesting he'd welcome such activity.

"I hope not, boy," the bearded hootowl replied,
reaching for another carbine still in its scabbard.

"That means we've got something in common,
friend," the Gunsmith announced as he stepped into the
open, pointing his pistol at the pair. "I'd just as soon we
don't have any shooting either. If you fellows will just
drop your guns and do as I tell you, there won't be any."

When Clint saw the wild expression in the kid's big
blue eyes, he knew there'd be bloodshed. The boy must
have figured the odds were about even since he had a
gun in his hands, already cocked and ready to be fired.
Uttering a strange sound, half gasp and half giggle, the
kid swung the muzzle of his carbine toward Clint and
braced the butt stock against his hip.

The Gunsmith's Colt roared. A big .45 caliber slug
plowed into the youngster's chest, the force of the heavy
projectile knocking him backward to collide with the
flanks of one of the horses. His Winchester clattered to
the ground, unfired. The boy's mouth hung open as he
sank to his knees. His eyes were filled with the amazed
expression of a fresh corpse—which was exactly what
he'd become. Then he fell forward, face first.

Moe had already started to whirl when the kid made
his move. He was still drawing a .44 Remington revolver
from its holster when Clint's weapon boomed again.
Moe cried out, his fingers flying from the butt of his holstered pistol as if it had just tried to bite him. His body

hurtled back into the brick wall of the bank. Clint stared at the man's clenched teeth, starkly visible in the center of his thick black beard, and watched his left hand slowly move toward the bullet would in his right shoulder.

"You're lucky you're slow, friend," the Gunsmith remarked. "Otherwise I wouldn't have had time to take such careful aim."

Moe may not have been much with a gun, but he was a bear of a man with the endurance of a young bull—and he proved he wasn't much smarter than one by going for the Remington with his left hand. Clint even had time to cock the Colt before he fired a third round. The bearded outlaw bellowed in agony when the next .45 slug struck the point of his left elbow, shattering bone and cartilage to pop the joint apart.

The outlaw dropped to one knee, both arms dangling uselessly. Sweat poured down his brow, forming a dew on the hairs of his beard. With his right collarbone broken, his left arm shattered and two bullets in him, Moe didn't present much of a threat. The Gunsmith walked around the dazed and wounded outlaw, confident he wouldn't be going very far in his condition.

"I'll be damned," Moe muttered thickly. His eyes rolled up into his head and he passed out.

"Not for a while anyway," Clint remarked as he moved to the mouth of the alley at the opposite side of the bank.

Although he'd hoped to capture the two outlaws stationed at the rear of the building without firing a shot, Clint had realized they might not prove obliging. When Clem Burns and the fourth member of the gang heard the shooting, Clint figured they would bolt from the bank, with or without the money. Since there were two men and only one horse hitched in front, they'd be counting on Moe and the kid bringing the rest of the mounts.

Obviously, that wouldn't happen now. So the pair would find themselves staring into Sheriff Wilson's rifle and either surrender or both try to escape on one horse. The situation seemed destined to take care of itself from that point on.

The Gunsmith heard boots pounding the plankwalk at the front of the building, which probably meant the outlaws had emerged from the bank, but he didn't hear Wilson order the men to surrender or any gunshots. In Texas, half the citizens should be pouring out into the street to back up the law. Clint frowned, wondering what had happened that he'd failed to consider.

Slowly, his Colt held ready, the Gunsmith started to move up through the alley. He saw a number of men standing across the street by the sheriff's office. Although armed with an assortment of handguns, shotguns and rifles, they merely stared at the bank, anger and frustration etched on their faces.

The reason for this suddenly stepped into view. Clem Burns held a young blond girl from behind, one thick arm wrapped around her waist while he pressed the muzzle of his revolver against the side of her head.

"That's it," the outlaw boss croaked in his hoarse Alabama voice. "You all just hold off or I blow this gal's pretty little haid off!"

Without warning, the remaining gang member swung into the alley, no doubt to see if he could retrieve one of the horses for their escape. He came to an abrupt halt when he suddenly came face to face with the Gunsmith.

The outlaw already had a Smith & Wesson .44 in his hand, so he reacted in an expected manner: He immediately tried to aim his revolver at Clint and shoot him. Clint didn't have any choice except to reply to the reaction in a like manner—and he was a hell of a lot faster than his opponent.

The Colt cracked while Hal was still trying to thumb back the hammer of his weapon. He fell against the side of the bank and blinked in surprise. Then he glanced down at the bloodstain that spread across the center of his checkered shirt. He realized he was dead just before his heart stopped to make the decision official.

When he heard the shot, Clem Burns, still holding his hostage, whirled to stare into the alley. He saw his partner's corpse slumped against the wall of the bank and the Gunsmith with his smoking Colt .45 pointed in his direction.

"Let her go, Burns," Clint told him in a flat, hard, authoritative voice.

"You drop your gun or I'll kill her!" the outlaw snarled in reply.

Clint saw the panic in Burns's eyes, which bulged from their sockets like the bullfrog he ressembled both physically and verbally. In his distressed state, Burns might indeed put a bullet in the girl's head, which would be an extreme pity. She was very pretty, with a clear alabaster complexion and lovely features, even though, at the moment, they were distorted by fear. Her body, clad in a blue gingham dress, promised to be as sweet as her face, although Clint barely allowed himself a fleeting glance. Distractions and gunfighting go together even worse than distractions and cards.

"I'm not going to drop my gun," Clint told Burns. "And you're not going to kill her either."

"You better do like I say—" Burns began.

"I'm going to count to three," Clint cut him off. "If you haven't released that girl and dropped your gun by then"—he shrugged—"I'll kill you."

The outlaw bit his lip, uncertain of what to do.

"One," Clint cocked the hammer of his Colt to emphasize the word.

Burns eased the muzzle of his revolver away from the girl's head.

"Two," Clint stated, his arm and the fingers holding the Colt as steady as a boulder.

Suddenly, Burns thrust his arm over the girl's shoulder, pointing the gun at Clint, hoping to blast his adversary while still using the girl as a shield. The Gunsmith's pistol snarled and Clem Burns's head instantly snapped back as a .45 round drilled through the center of his forehead. The back of his skull exploded and a spray of pink and gray matter spewed out of his head. His gun arm rose with the sudden violent jerk of his body and the revolver in his hand discharged harmlessly into the sky. Burns's other arm fell away from the girl's trim waist a moment before his body crashed to the ground.

"Three," the Gunsmith sighed as he holstered his weapon.

THREE

The citizens of Brownsville were eager to express their gratitude to Clint Adams for preventing the bank robbery. Two of the local diners offered him free meals for as long as he stayed in town. One hotel extended a similar invitation, but limited the expense-free room to three days and nights. Several shop owners told him to stop by and help himself to whatever he'd like—no charge.

All of this was a bit too much for Clint. Naturally he appreciated their gratitude, but he'd always been one to pay his own way and he'd never been comfortable in the limelight. His current financial hardships made the offers tempting, yet it also made him feel that accepting them would be a form of charity under the circumstances.

"I didn't do this because I wanted to be rewarded for it," the Gunsmith told the crowd that had gathered around him in the street. He felt embarrassingly like a preacher at a revival addressing his congregation.

"All the more reason why you should be," the portly owner of a haberdashery declared. Several others voiced their approval of this logic.

"I really can't accept—" Clint began.

"Come on, mister," the bartender who'd been so surly before urged. "You ain't gonna offend us by refusing our hospitality, are you?"

15

Clint grinned. The irony of the situation stunned him. He'd come to Brownsville because he was down on his luck and now everybody was offering more than he could accept.

"All right," he sighed. "How about a compromise? If any of you folks want to give me a discount on anything I buy, that's fine, but you don't have to feel obliged to do so, and I won't take anything for free."

Most of the crowd didn't seem to think this was quite good enough. Others seemed to feel it was reasonable and a few appeared to be downright relieved. Somebody asked if he couldn't at least buy Clint a beer and half a dozen other men quickly added their desire to do likewise.

"Hold on," Clint laughed. "You'll turn me into a drunk. Before I do anything else, I've got to see to my horses and rig. Oh, yeah. If any of you happen to have a gun that needs some repairs or modifications, that's how I make my living, and I'd welcome your business while I'm in Brownsville."

"Then what the sheriff said is the truth," a voice remarked, a trace of awe in its tone. "You're the Gunsmith, ain't you?"

"I'm Clint Adams."

"However you want it, Clint," a beefy, red-haired man replied. "Just remember when you're ready to be gettin' a room here in town to come on over to the Shamrock Hotel."

Several others added their offers for accommodations and goods—and the young whore who'd noticed Clint from the saloon window told him she'd give him a good price for some special services. The Gunsmith managed to work his way through the congregation, receiving enough pats on the back and shaking enough hands to feel like a politician running for office.

Finally, he headed toward the livery to see to Duke and his other two horses and the equipment he'd left on the wagon. He almost reached his goal when Sheriff Matt Wilson approached him.

"Really appreciate how you helped take care of things today, Clint," the lawman told him.

"Glad to be of assistance, Sheriff."

"Yeah, well . . ." Wilson began awkwardly. "I'm just wonderin' why you did it."

"You shouldn't have to ask that question, Sheriff," Clint replied dryly. "Not if you're wearing that star on your chest for the right reasons."

FOUR

The accommodations provided by the Shamrock Hotel proved to be quite adequate, consisting of a bed, a chest of drawers and a small wooden table with a chair, a wash basin and a coal-oil lamp. Clint felt pleasantly weary by the time he entered the hotel room and tossed his stetson on the bed.

He'd eaten a big steak-and-potatoes dinner for three cents, enjoyed a long hot bath in a barber shop after a shave and a haircut—all for a nickel—and then visited the saloon and allowed four men to buy him beers. Deciding that was a reasonable amount of brew for one night, he'd declined several more offers and headed for the Shamrock.

Clint struck a match and lit the lamp. Although he felt tired enough to go to bed, he made room at the table to work and removed a small revolver wrapped in oilcloth from his pocket.

Harry Collins, the barber, had turned out to be Clint's only customer so far, although several others told him they'd be bringing him guns to work on the following morning. The Gunsmith unwrapped the oilcloth and examined the barber's .32 Smith & Wesson pocket pistol.

"Harry tells me he can't cock you," Clint spoke to the gun as though it could understand him. He had a habit of talking to guns and horses—especially Duke. Clint didn't see anything wrong with this; he figured he'd start to worry when they started talking back.

He tried the hammer gingerly and discovered reasonable thumb pressure wouldn't budge it. Clint made a guess about the problem with the pistol and reached under the table for a box containing some of his gunsmithing tools.

Selecting a small screwdriver, he removed the walnut grips of the little S&W and silently congratulated himself on guessing correctly. The hammer bar and spring were shrouded by a dark, gumlike substance.

"Harry's been oiling you a bit too often and then storing you away somewhere that's too dusty," Clint remarked, taking the parts out and cleaning them with a cloth. "Better check your trigger mechanism while I'm—"

Knuckles rapped gently on the door. Clint's hand automatically moved to his hip and draped the butt of his holstered Colt as he rose from the chair.

"Come in," he invited.

The door opened and the blond girl Clint had rescued stood at the threshold. He smiled at her and she returned the gesture with a sheepish grin.

"I—" she began, "I thought I heard you talking to someone."

"Just thinking out loud," he replied, aware that the answer sounded less loco than admitting to a one-way conversation with a .32 Smith & Wesson.

The girl stepped inside and eased the door shut. "I wanted to thank you for what you did today."

Clint noticed that she'd closed the door, but he didn't jump to any conclusions. "No need for that, ma'am," he assured her. "But you're more than welcome anyway."

"Oh, my name is Loretta Baiser," she said.

Clint could take time to get a better look at her now

that he didn't have to contend with an armed outlaw at the same time. Her large blue eyes were definitely come-hither and her lips formed a tempting bow.

"Your name suits you," Clint remarked.

"Loretta?"

"Baiser," he explained. "Isn't that French for kiss?"

The girl smiled and stepped closer. "Do you speak French, Clint?"

"No," he replied. "But I kiss in several different languages."

"Show me," Loretta invited, her arms reaching for Clint's neck.

The Gunsmith embraced her and drew his mouth close to hers. She closed her eyes and prepared to receive his kiss, but Clint slowly extended the tip of his tongue and ran it along her lips instead. The girl trembled with pleasure until she crushed her lips against his.

Clint's tongue continued probing inside her mouth. He resisted an urge to explore her body with his hands until he felt her grind her pelvis against his crotch. His fingers then deftly stroked her back and neck.

Slowly, Loretta broke the embrace and reached her arms back to unfasten her dress. Although Clint's manhood swelled in expectation, he lived by certain principles. He knew if he didn't he'd have trouble living with himself.

"Loretta, you don't have to thank me *that* much."

She looked at him, a trace of surprise and hurt in her expression. "You mean you don't want to?"

"Of course I want to," Clint assured her. "I mean I'm only going to be in Brownsville for a few days and then I'll be moving on—alone. It's my way, Loretta. I want you to realize that before you say or do anything else."

Loretta smiled. "That's considerate, Clint," she said. "And I appreciate your honesty."

Then she continued to take off her clothes. The Gunsmith followed her example. They frankly admired each other's bodies. Loretta nodded with satisfaction at the sight of Clint's leanly muscled physique. He somehow seemed bigger without clothes on, due to the muscular development of his chest and shoulders.

Clint's gaze roamed down the girl's swanlike white neck to the splendor of her breasts, capped by firm, stiff nipples. Her waist was narrow and her softly rounded hips tapered into long creamy thighs. The Gunsmith didn't allow his gaze to linger on the tawny patch of hair between them.

Loretta, however, had no hesitation about examining his genitals. The girl sank to her knees and eagerly licked his erection before slipping her lips over its head. She cupped his testicles in her hands as she drew her mouth to and fro along the length of his fleshy shaft.

She's French, sure enough, Clint thought as hot pleasure filled his loins.

The girl almost brought him to the limit before she rose and moved to the bed. Clint followed, easing her back onto the mattress. His lips gently kissed her neck and she gasped when the tip of his tongue massaged the hollow of her throat. At the same time, Clint's fingers found one of her breasts. He fondled it tenderly, thumbing the nipple until it stood hard and erect.

Clint's mouth took his hand's place as the fingers traveled down her belly to her thighs. Slowly, his touch moved to her pubic hair. The girl spread her legs to receive his stroking fingers. He began to work his lips down her abdomen.

"No need for that, Clint," Loretta cooed. "I'm ready. God, am I ready!"

So was Clint. He mounted the woman's gorgeous, eager body. She didn't want to waste any time. He'd barely climbed into position before she'd taken his erection in hand and guided it inside her. The Gunsmith eased his penis deeper by rotating his hips, working his organ into her with tantalizing slowness.

"More!" she pleaded. "Give me every inch!"

And he gave it to her, a little at a time. He paced himself carefully, slowly increasing the speed and penetration of his thrusts. Loretta's body began to buck wildly. She bit into his shoulder when her moans of pleasure became uncontrollable. Clint immediately increased the tempo.

"O-o-oh that feels go-o-od!" she cried, reaching an orgasm.

Clint kissed and fondled her as he slowly began the cycle of gradual thrusts a second time. This time she came rather quickly. He repeated the procedure a third time, feeling himself rapidly near his brink.

"Oh, God!" Loretta cried in delight and amazement. "Again?"

"I'm trying," he replied through clenched teeth, straining to hold his load as her body responded to his ramming manhood.

Then he exploded inside her. The girl's legs wrapped around his torso as she convulsed beneath him. His throbbing organ still managed to carry her a third time into sensual ecstasy.

"You are quite a man, Clint Adams," Loretta Baiser sighed.

A few minutes later, they started all over again and Clint decided she was quite a woman as well.

FIVE

Although sexually willing and bold enough to go to bed with the Gunsmith on the very day they met, Loretta was still concerned enough about her reputation in Brownsville not to want to spend the night in his hotel room. Two hours after she'd arrived, the girl kissed him good-bye and left.

Clint drifted into a deep, blissful sleep only to have it disturbed by a loud pounding at the door. He awoke with a start, reaching for his gunbelt draped over the headboard of the bed. Drawing the modified Colt, he sat up and allowed his eyes to adjust to the darkness.

"Adams?" a deep, authoritative voice demanded. "Are you too damn drunk to answer me, Adams?"

"I'm cold sober and wide awake," Clint replied gruffly. "And you don't sound like you're worth losing any sleep to meet."

"I can kick the door in if'n you want, Mr. Mather," an arrogant, slightly nasal voice remarked.

"That's a good way for a man to get his head blown off," the Gunsmith said sharply as he climbed out of bed and pulled on his trousers.

The snide voice chuckled in response. "Feller must figure he's pretty tough, Mr. Mather."

"That's why I want to talk to him, Lloyd," the first voice declared.

"Then let's talk," Clint said, turning the key in the lock. "But make it brief and keep it friendly."

The door swung open. A coal-oil lamp in the hallway formed the silhouettes of the two figures, one tall and heavily built with a white stetson on top. The other man was short and wiry with a *sombrero de corta* flat-crowned hat on his head. Neither had a weapon in hand. Clint kept his Colt ready nonetheless as he crossed the room and lit the lamp on his table.

Yellow light illuminated the features of his visitors. The large man's face was tanned and deeply lined, suggesting constant exposure to weather. His features were Nordic—a straight nose, lantern jaw and pale blue eyes. He wore a checkered shirt with a string tie, clean denim trousers and boots in good condition. Even the white stetson on his gray-haired head was unstained by sweat or dirt.

His companion's face resembled an inverted triangle. The man's features were sharp—a needle nose, pointed chin and small white teeth between thin, colorless lips. Dark blond hair, like dirty straw, extended from his black Mexican rancher's hat to the collar of a soiled white shirt. He wore black leather pants and a matching vest. A low-hung holster on his left hip contained a .44 Remington with a modified backsight for additional accuracy and an extra-wide hammer for greater speed in cocking the single-action pistol.

A gunhawk, Clint thought. *He might as well wear a sign around his neck announcing it to the world.*

"Perhaps we should start with an introduction," the first man began, wasting no time on apologizing for waking Clint. "My name is Jacob Mather. I own one of the largest ranches in this county. Basically, I raise cattle, but I also breed horses. Both have proven quite profitable."

"Maybe you've got the wrong room," Clint sighed. "I'm not a writer for an Eastern newspaper, so I'm really not all that excited about hearing your success story."

"Got a big mouth, don't he?" the wiry man snorted. He glared at Clint. "Maybe I oughtta learn you some manners."

"We didn't come here so you two could see who's faster with a gun," Mather snapped.

"Why are you here?" Clint demanded. Neither of the two men had done anything to make him welcome their visit and his normally even temper was rapidly reaching a boiling point.

"Why, I've come to hire the Gunsmith, of course," Mather smiled.

"You want a gun repaired"—Clint shrugged—"see me tomorrow."

"Everybody knows you're more famous for using a gun than tinkering with them," Mather snorted. "Your heroics this afternoon prove that you haven't lost your touch. Why, you and Stansfield Lloyd here are probably the best gunmen in the West."

"Stansfield Lloyd?" Clint raised his eyebrows.

The wiry man in black smiled. "Heard of me, eh?"

"Yeah," the Gunsmith admitted. He hadn't cared much for what he'd heard. Lloyd was a mercenary: Anybody could hire him if they had enough money, and he wasn't particular if he drew on a dirt farmer or a professional pistolman. However, he'd beaten enough of the latter in fair face-to-face confrontations to prove he was fast and deadly with a gun.

"If you've got him"—Clint tilted his head toward Lloyd—"what do you need me for?"

"My daughter is engaged to a fine young man in Yuma," Mather began, removing a stogie from his shirt pocket. "The train Linda will be on will travel through

Texas and New Mexico to the Arizona Territory. As I'm sure you realize, that's probably the wildest, most dangerous territory in the Southwest. Most of it is Apache country. Have you ever had any run-ins with the Apache, Adams?"

"Enough not to want to have another one," Clint confessed.

"You afraid of the Apache, Adams?" Lloyd snickered.

"*You'd* better be if you're going into their territory," the Gunsmith replied.

"If you don't have the guts for the job . . ." Lloyd began.

"I'll decide who I hire," Mather said sternly.

"And I'll decide if I'll accept or not," Clint added.

"Here's my offer, Adams," the rancher said, striking a match on the side of the door to light his cigar. "I'll pay you three thousand dollars to serve on the escort team to protect my daughter during the trip."

"Three thousand dollars?" the Gunsmith couldn't help finding the offer attractive when he only had fifty dollars left in his bankroll.

"Half now and half when my daughter arrives in Yuma."

"Who'll be in charge of the team?" Clint inquired.

"Me," Lloyd smiled.

The Gunsmith shrugged. "I'll take the job anyway."

"Good," Mather said, extracting a gold-plated pocket watch from his trousers. "It's three twenty. Get your gear together. We've arranged for a boxcar to transport your horses and wagon. The train leaves at dawn."

SIX

Excited shouts of encouragement and groans of disgust mingled with the sound of fists striking flesh. Clint Adams, Jacob Mather and Stansfield Lloyd heard the commotion as they approached the train. Mather shook his head with despair.

"Bruno is showing off again," he muttered.

"He's a good man, Mr. Mather," Lloyd remarked. "Just a little high-spirited at times."

"Bruno?" the Gunsmith inquired, leading Duke by his reins. A group of railroad personnel would see to getting his wagon and team into a boxcar, but Clint insisted on taking care of his prize black gelding himself.

"He'll be one of your traveling companions," Mather explained. "Vargas and Markham are probably watching the show. You may as well meet everyone now."

They walked around the wide cowcatcher of the locomotive engine to the other side of the train. A group of men had gathered along the boxcars to watch as three combatants fought by torchlight. Most of the spectators wore dungarees and caps. None of the railroad personnel seemed pleased by the bare-knuckled contest. However, two onlookers laughed heartily as the battle neared its climax.

All three men involved in the brawl were large and

well muscled, but Clint assumed Bruno was the hulking brute with a shaven head who grinned as he sent one of the dungaree-clad opponents to the ground with a right cross. He was stripped to the waist, his big biceps and triceps bulging under his skin like the coils of a great serpent. Bruno's chest was as big as a keg of nails and his shoulders were almost a yard wide.

The third combatant was taller than the bald man, although not as thickly muscled. He seized Bruno from behind, but the brute simply shook him off and swung the back of his fist into the taller man's face, knocking him to the ground.

The first adversary rose and slammed a solid punch to Bruno's jaw. His bald head hardly moved from the blow and he immediately drove a fist into the other man's stomach. The railroad worker doubled up with a groan and Bruno sent him sprawling with a left hook to the side of the head.

Snarling with rage, the second fighter launched himself at Bruno. The bald man still smiled. He caught the hurtling form in his massive hands and raised the startled man overhead as though he were a bag of grain. The unfortunate fellow screamed as Bruno savagely dashed him to the ground. The man's back hit the earth hard. He moaned once, then lay still.

Slowly, the first man rose to his hands and knees. "I give up," he rasped breathlessly.

"You sure?" Bruno inquired, stepping closer.

He viciously kicked the man in the face. The vanquished opponent collapsed and lay unconscious, his jaw broken.

"There weren't no need for him to do that!" one of the railroad men snapped.

"That so?" This from a husky individual with a dark complexion and oily black hair that flowed from a straw sombrero to his shoulders; Clint correctly guessed he was Vargas. The man pointed at Bruno with the blade of a fancy ivory-handled dagger. "Maybe you like to teach him some manners, no?"

The protester shook his head.

"Shit," a skinny young man who Clint assumed to be Markham snorted. He was dressed in a flashy red and yellow shirt, denim trousers, and boots with big silver spurs. The gunbelt around his narrow waist held twin Army Colts holstered to each hip. "Bruno took on both your men at the same time and whupped 'em. Don't bitch about how he done it." The youth's hands draped the butts of his pistols to accent the warning.

"You *hombres* bet on your boys and they lost," the swarthy man remarked, tossing the knife in his hand to deftly catch it by the tip of the blade. "Now pay up!"

Without further warning, Vargas threw the dagger. It whistled between the heads of two spectators and slammed, point first, into the side of a wooden boxcar. The railroad workers gasped in alarm. The knife thrower, his young companion and Bruno laughed at their startled expressions.

"Well, Adams," Mather commented with a grin. "Meet the rest of the team."

"Wonderful," Clint replied dryly.

Every instinct told him to quit and walk away from the job, but the fifteen hundred dollars in his pocket and the promise of another fat payment when they reached Yuma were powerful incentives to stay.

Oh, well, the Gunsmith thought. *Just how bad can the trip be?*

SEVEN

The Gunsmith, Jacob Mather and Stansfield Lloyd climbed onto the train. Entering a passenger car, the rancher led them through the corridors. Coal-oil lanterns mounted on the walls illuminated the narrow hallway. Clint Adams glanced about the interior with admiration. The car was first class all the way. Flowery wallpaper and a blue carpet created a hotel atmosphere. The tinplated ceiling reflected the lamplight effectively dispelling the darkness.

"You'll get to know your . . . colleagues better during the trip," Mather declared.

"Yeah," Clint replied without enthusiasm. He'd already seen enough to know Lloyd, Vargas, Bruno and Markham weren't the kind of people he wanted to form friendships with, but this was business and the Gunsmith had worked with men he didn't like in the past—and often for a lot less than three thousand dollars.

"However," the rancher continued, "I feel I should introduce you to Linda personally."

They approached a door marked 12. Mather lightly rapped his knuckles on it. "Linda?"

"Daddy?" a feminine voice replied.

"Yes, dear," he confirmed. "I'd like you to meet a new member of the team who will be traveling with you to Yuma."

The door opened and a young woman appeared. Her blue cotton dress didn't conceal the intriguing curves of her tall, lovely figure. Clint subtly examined the girl with an appreciative eye. Linda's oval face was smooth and without blemish, framed by long locks of auburn hair. Her eyes were more green than blue with long curved lashes.

"Linda," Mather began, placing a hand on her shoulder. "This is Clint Adams, better known as the Gunsmith."

"Oh?" she cocked a frail eyebrow with interest. "The same Gunsmith we've heard so many stories about?"

"When I hire protection for my only daughter," the rancher said, "I hire the best."

"Well, I'm impressed, Daddy," Linda's wide, sensuous mouth smiled, but her tone was somewhat sarcastic. She turned to face Clint. "I certainly never expected to meet the Gunsmith. What an unexpected surprise."

"Please call me Clint," he replied. "And the pleasure is all mine, ma'am. May I say you're the best-looking company I've met on this train."

"Why, thank you, Clint," the girl smiled and nodded.

Mather frowned. Stansfield Lloyd glared at the Gunsmith, but Clint was more interested in the girl's reaction than their opinion. She assessed his appearance with obvious approval and gazed intently into his dark brown eyes with bold interest.

The rancher gripped Linda's shoulder firmly, almost roughly. "Go and rest now, dear," he said, a trace of gruffness in his tone. "We men have business to discuss."

"Whatever you say, Daddy," she answered lightly, in a manner just short of mocking her parent.

The girl returned to her room and closed the door. A dark emotional cloud seemed to cover Jacob Mather's features as he turned to Clint.

"You've got something of a reputation for being as handy with the ladies as you are with a gun, Adams," he began. "So let me impress upon you that you're here to guard my daughter on this trip and that's *all* you'd better do!"

"Flattering a pretty woman is sort of a habit of mine," Clint shrugged.

"That might not be such a healthy habit to have, Adams," Lloyd hissed.

"Linda is engaged to be married," Mather said. "She's spoken for. Don't forget that."

"So I won't say anything nice to her," Clint sighed. "Just what *am* I supposed to do?"

"Lloyd will tell you your duties," the rancher answered. "And remember: *He's* in charge."

"I reckon I can remind him if'n he forgets," the pistolman smiled.

"I bet," Clint muttered.

"Any questions, Adams?" Mather demanded.

"Only one," the Gunsmith replied. "I'll get the rest of my money in Yuma, right?"

"That's what we agreed on," the rancher nodded.

"Who will pay me?"

"Linda has the money," Mather told him. "Don't get any ideas about *that* either."

Clint clucked his tongue against the roof of his mouth with disgust. "If you don't trust me, Mather, why'd you hire me?" he inquired.

"For your ability with a gun," the rancher replied flatly. "Not your honesty. Although, from what I've heard about you and judging from what happened yesterday, I'd say you're not a thief, just a killer."

"Every man is a lot of things," the Gunsmith stated, "depending on the circumstances he finds himself in."

EIGHT

Stansfield Lloyd addressed Clint Adams and the other three members of the escort team in a passenger car after Jacob Mather left the train. The Gunsmith noticed the majority of the seats were empty. Obviously, train travel in the Southwest wasn't popular. Not surprising since bands of Apache, Comanche, Kiowa and other hostile Indian tribes had recently been raiding settlers and small units of cavalry from Texas to the Arizona Territory.

The Gunsmith observed some of his fellow passengers. A portly man in a three-piece Eastern suit, totally out of place for the climate, sat opposite a gaunt minister. A tall raw-boned Texan and a plump woman were seated across from three sleepy-eyed children. All of them seemed to be purposely avoiding contact with Linda Mather's escort team.

Others were no doubt in their quarters, either sleeping or unpacking for the trip. Clint wondered why these people had decided to take such a damn fool journey through dangerous Indian territory. *They probably have their reasons and they'd probably feel theirs are better than mine for being here,* he thought. *And maybe they'd be right.*

"Listen up," Lloyd began. "You fellers know why you're here. We got a job to do and we're gonna do it right."

"Sure," Markham grinned as he twirled one of his Colt revolvers on his trigger finger. "If'n any of those red niggers are stupid enough to attack this train, we kill 'em. Simple enough."

"Don't interrupt me, Jimmy," Lloyd growled.

"Jimmy," Clint said in a hard voice. "That gun isn't a toy. Put it away before you have an accident with it."

Markham grinned without humor and tapped his chin with the barrel of his Colt. "And what do you reckon to do if'n I don't, Gunsmith?"

Clint sighed. The youngster needed somebody to teach him a lesson in manners as well as common sense. Sooner or later somebody would and the kid would probably die in the process, but Clint guessed there'd be enough opportunities for trouble on the trip without encouraging any with Markham or the others.

"I'm talkin', damn it!" Lloyd snapped. "But Adams is right, Jimmy. Shut up and quit playin' with that gun like you was a baby with a rattle, for crissake."

"Sure, Stan," the kid nodded and sullenly holstered his revolver. "Just you tell this Gunsmith feller not to try 'n' ride herd on me."

"I'm right here, Jim," Clint informed him. "You don't need any messengers. I just don't like seeing somebody mishandle a firearm. Keep it in the holster until you intend to use it. Fair enough?"

"All right," Lloyd continued. "You fellers are all aware of the fact this train is goin' through some mighty mean country."

"Hell, Stan," Bruno muttered. The burly man now wore a checkered shirt and a gunbelt with a .44 Smith & Wesson in a belly holster. "None of those injuns are gonna be crazy enough to attack a big ol' iron horse like this rig."

"Apache are loco enough to attack anything," Vargas commented, lighting a black cheroot.

"The redskins ain't the only thing we have to worry about," Lloyd added. "This train will be travelin' close to the border and a big enough gang of Mex bandits might figure we'd be an easy target."

"That's possible," Clint allowed. "But I think any *bandidos* would figure we might be full of troops being transferred to cavalry posts. I don't imagine they'd run the risk of tangling with us for that reason."

"You willing to bet your life on that, Adams?" Lloyd challenged.

"I said it's *possible*," the Gunsmith explained. "I just don't think it's very likely."

"Unlikely things happen, feller," Markham sneered. His hands were draped over the grips of his Colts as he glared at Clint.

"That's a fact," the Gunsmith admitted.

"Of course," Lloyd said. "Our main concern is to see to it nothing happens to Miss Mather. That's why we're gonna take turns guardin' her door."

Clint raised his eyebrows with surprise. Posting sentries around the clock seemed extreme to the Gunsmith, but he didn't voice his opinion.

"You fellers will be broken into shifts—six hours each. First Bruno, then Jimmy, then Mike and then our new addition, Adams here. Any questions?"

"What happened to your shift, Stan?" Vargas asked, resentment in his voice.

"I ain't takin' one," the gunfighter answered. "I'm in charge of the rest of you. That means I'll be checkin' to make sure you all stand your guard proper. If I catch anybody asleep or drunk on duty, I'll toss him off this train next stop it makes . . . unless I decide not to wait that long."

"Nobody gets thrown off this train without my say-so!" a gruff voice declared.

They turned to face the speaker, a short, thickly built

man with a small scrub-brush mustache. Dressed in a
white shirt, suit trousers and a vest with a gold watch
chain extended across his broad belly, he would have resembled a prosperous businessman if he didn't have a
.44 Hopkins & Allen on his hip.

"Who are you, feller?" Lloyd demanded, his tone
suggesting he didn't really care.

"I'm Walter Patterson, Pinkerton Detective," the
man replied with a pompous jerk of his head to arro-
gantly lift his double chin. "I'm in charge of law and order on this train."

"Ain't that something," Bruno remarked, cracking
his knuckles to add menace to his contempt. "Just like
in the dime novels, huh?"

"We don't reckon we have any business with you,"
Lloyd stated. "You figure you got any with us?"

"I see you men as potential troublemakers," the
Pinkerton man answered. "You've got hardcase written
all over you—all five of you!"

The pistolman glared at Patterson. Vargas and Bruno
grinned while Markham's chest seemed to swell with
pride. Clint gave a small, helpless shrug.

"If I have any trouble with you," Patterson continued, "I'll have this train stopped, wherever we happen
to be at the time, and you'll be allowed to get your horses out of the cattle cars and then you'll be on your own.
Is that understood?"

"We've got a job to do," Lloyd replied flatly.

"This man is just trying to do his," the Gunsmith stated. "I'll admit none of us are exactly choirboys," he told
the detective. "But we're on this train to stop trouble,
not to start it, Mr. Patterson."

"Well, see to it you behave," the Pinkerton man
snorted before he waddled away.

"*Cabrón*," Vargas muttered sourly.

"We didn't have to give that son of a bitch no explanations," Markham looked at Clint with contempt. "Why didn't you kiss him while you were at it, Adams?"

The Gunsmith sighed. "There's no point in getting on bad terms with the man. We'd do better if we tried to get along with him, wouldn't we?"

"Adams is right." Lloyd grinned. "Let the fat man swagger around and enjoy himself—so long as he don't get in our way."

The others smiled. A large, cold knot formed in Clint's stomach. He felt as though he was the only wolf in the pack that didn't have rabies. The screech of a whistle announced that the train was about to move. It seemed to mock the Gunsmith for his decision to remain with the group as the locomotive lurched forward.

NINE

The Gunsmith carried his gear into his quarters. The room was a small, stuffy compartment with two bunks mounted doubledecker style to the wall. Mike Vargas sat on the bottom mattress, honing his knife with a stone. He looked up at Clint with disinterest and continued to sharpen his dagger.

"Guess Stan put you in here with me," he muttered. "Figures."

"Yeah," Clint said dryly. "I'm just thrilled to have you for a roommate too."

Vargas rose and pointed the tip of his knife at Clint. "You don't like sharing quarters with a half-breed, no?" He gestured with the dagger. "You want to do somethin' about it?"

Clint's left hand lowered his saddlebags to the floor as his right fell to the holstered .45 on his hip. "Relax, Vargas. You'll live longer. Besides, I figure I have to room with one of you guys. Lloyd has a room to himself and I don't imagine I'd care much for his company anyway. Markham would probably be just as bad and Bruno doesn't seem like such a great fellow either. Right now, all I have against you is the fact you seem aweful eager to use that knife when there's no need for it."

"I am very good with a knife, Adams," Vargas

smiled, but he backed away from the Gunsmith and sat on the bunk. "I had to learn how to use a blade as a boy because everybody hates a mixed blood like me. I have used a knife many times in the past and I've killed a lot of men with one, Adams."

"I believe you," Clint nodded. "Guess I get the top bunk, right?"

"*Sí*," Vargas gestured with his dagger again. "Any objections?"

"No," Clint assured him, shoving his gear in a corner.

"You're a real obliging *hombre*, aren't you?" Vargas remarked. His tone suggested he found the characteristic to be a weakness.

"I try to be," the Gunsmith answered as he climbed onto the top bunk.

"You know something, Adams?"

"A couple of things," Clint replied, stretching out on the mattress.

"I'm not just a half-breed," Vargas said bitterly. "I ain't that lucky."

"How's that?" Clint said. He didn't really care, but Vargas obviously wanted to talk and the Gunsmith hoped the conversation would discourage the man from getting any more notions about his knife.

"My father was part Yaqui Indian. In *Mejico* that's the same as being a leper. He crossed the border and got married to another outcast. My mother was half-Anglo and half-colored. I guess one of those plantation fieldhands got himself one of those lily-white Southern *putas* or a planter did some late-night plowin' with a nigger maid. Ma never explained how it happened. Maybe she didn't know herself.

"So I wind up with all four races in my veins," Vargas continued. Clint heard him rummage about under his bunk and then pull the cork from a bottle, probably tequila or whiskey. "Do you know what it's like being half-gringo, half-greaser, half-injun and half-nigger?"

"That's a lot of halves."

"What's that?"

"No, I guess I don't."

"No, you have no idea because you are an Anglo," Vargas growled. "It is hell for one that is less than pure white to live in this country."

Clint didn't comment. If Vargas wanted to wallow in self-pity, the Gunsmith figured that was his privilege.

Suddenly, Vargas laughed. "But money is the great equalizer. One day I will be very rich and then the *gringos* will treat me with respect. You speak like a man educated in the East. They taught you to talk good and act like a gentleman, no? You probably read books and write letters and you think that makes you better than me."

"Vargas" Clint replied in a weary voice, "I don't think I'm any better than you and I haven't done anything to merit your accusations. We're supposed to be here to protect Mather's daughter, not to fight among ourselves."

"*Sí*," Vargas laughed bitterly. "You talk good, Adams, but why are you with us, eh?"

"I keep asking myself the same question," Clint sighed. "I think it had something to do with money."

"*Sí*," Vargas barked with delight. "It is what I said, no? Money and power. That's all the Anglos admire. One day, I will have plenty of both."

With that, Vargas turned his attention to his bottle. He didn't offer to share his liquor with the Gunsmith, which didn't bother Clint. The Gunsmith kept his pistol by his side, hand resting on the butt, in case Vargas got crazy drunk and decided to cut him up just because he was available. However, the mixed breed only drank for a while, muttered something in Spanish that Clint didn't understand and lay down on his bunk. Clint soon heard snoring coming from the bottom cot.

Clint glanced down at his gear in the corner and decided he'd have to fish the .22 New Line Colt revolver out of the saddlebags when he got a chance to do so without Vargas or any of the others being aware of it. The Gunsmith had picked up the diminutive gun in Kansas a while back and often carried it when he felt a backup weapon might be needed. Everything seemed to suggest his current adventure would get worse before it was over—and the very men he was working with promised to be a bigger threat than any band of Apaches they might encounter on the way to Yuma.

He stripped down to his long johns and closed his eyes. Clint allowed himself to drift into a light slumber, his senses still alert although his muscles and nervous system rested. He had slept in this manner most of his adult life, a weapon always within reach. At times, the Gunsmith wondered if he'd ever be able to fully relax.

When I'm dead, he thought.

The answer seemed logical enough and it didn't disturb his sleep.

TEN

A woman's scream jolted Clint from his shallow slumber. Fully alert and instantly aware of his surroundings, the Gunsmith leaped from the bunk and landed nimbly on his feet, the modified Colt in his fist. Clint jerked open the door and dashed from the room before Vargas had even risen from his cot.

The Gunsmith followed the woman's voice through the corridor. A middle-aged man's head poked from an open doorway, gazing curiously down the hall, although not quite curious enough to get personally involved. His eyes swelled in their sockets when he saw the tall figure of Clint Adams, clad only in his long johns, charging toward him with a gun in his hand. The man swiftly retreated into his quarters and slammed the door. The Gunsmith kept moving.

As he'd suspected, the scream had come from Linda Mather's room. *Where the hell is the sentry?* Clint thought, glancing about even as he ran, half-expecting to see the dead or unconscious figure of one of the escort team sprawled on the floor. *Worry about it later,* he told himself as he slammed a naked foot into the door.

It burst open and he immediately dropped to one knee and cocked the Colt, held in a firm two-handed grip. Jimmy Markham stared into the muzzle of Clint's gun. Linda Mather stood beside a large, brass-framed bed. She tried to hold together a negligee in one small fist. The front of the flimsy pink garment had been torn apart. Linda's other hand rubbed her right cheek. Both sides of her face were tinted crimson.

"I didn't hurt her!" Markham declared. Although he wore his twin Colts, both hands were raised in surrender.

"Are you all right, Miss Mather?" Clint asked, his gun still trained on the youth.

"Yes" she replied in an unsteady voice. "Just make him leave me alone." Linda tilted her head toward Markham.

"Looks to me like he tried to force himself on you and slapped you around to try to get you to oblige," the Gunsmith remarked, rising and walking into the room.

"She wouldn't stop screamin'," Markham declared as though to justify his actions. "I wouldn't have hit her if'n she'd been quiet."

"You little bastard," Clint hissed through clenched teeth.

"No!" Linda exclaimed. "Don't shoot him. Just get him out of here, please."

The Gunsmith approached Markham. "The lady thinks I should let you go, but I'm inclined to think you deserve a bullet. What do you think, kid?"

"Well," Markham thought for a second or two. "I didn't really do nothin' . . ."

"Oh?" Clint shrugged as he eased the hammer forward to uncock his Colt.

Markham began to lower his arms and sighed with relief. The exhaled air suddenly became a retching gasp when Clint rammed the muzzle of his pistol into the kid's solar plexus. His left hand turned into a fist and cracked into the side of Markham's skull, sending him into a corner.

"Pretty touch with a woman, huh?" Clint remarked, tossing his Colt onto the bed.

"He's still armed, Clint!" Linda cried in horror.

"So what?" the Gunsmith rasped as he stepped toward the young gunman.

Through a scarlet haze, Markham saw his opponent's hands were now empty. His lips twisted like snakes to form a sneer as his hands plunged to the butts of his holstered revolvers.

The Gunsmith's right leg swung out. He raised his toes to drive the hard ball of his bare foot into Markham's crotch. Agony shot through the boy's groin to branch out through his nervous system like an electrical shock. His mouth formed a black oval, but the only sound to escape from his throat was a dull gurgle.

His hands abandoned the still holstered pistols to claw at the source of his suffering between his legs. Clint whipped a right cross to the kid's jaw and propelled him into a fancy chest of drawers with a large mirror. An ivory-handled hair brush clattered to the floor as the impact of Markham's body rocked the furniture.

"*Madre de Dios!*" Vargas exclaimed. He'd arrived in time to see the Gunsmith discard his revolver and take on the young pistolman barehanded. "*Mucho machismo . . . mucho loco!*"

Markham staggered away from the dresser, his knees buckling slightly. Clint was a bit surprised that the kid was still on his feet. Oh, well. That could be taken care of easily enough.

Watching the Gunsmith's feet, Markham reached for his Colts once more. However, the kid had to get the guns out of leather before he could use them, something Clint didn't intend to allow. The Gunsmith quickly stepped forward and grabbed Markham's wrists, pinning his hands—and the revolvers—to the holsters.

Clint's head reared back and shot forward, the front of his skull butting Markham in the face. The youth sagged, blood trickling from his mouth and both nostrils. Clint pulled Markham's arms to draw the kid's Colts, then twisted the boy's wrists and forced the guns to fall from their owner's grasp.

An uppercut slammed into Markham's already battered solar plexus. The boy moaned as he doubled up. Clint seized the youth's hair with his left hand, jerked Markham's head back and delivered a devastating right to the point of the kid's jaw. Markham crashed to the floor.

"That's enough!" Stansfield Lloyd demanded. He and Bruno had joined Vargas in the doorway to witness the conclusion of the onesided battle.

"I think Jimmy would agree," Vargas commented. "If he could talk right now."

"Not bad, Adams," Bruno said, looking down at the unconscious youth.

"Jimmy was molesting me, Stan," Linda explained. "Clint came to my rescue." She turned to the Gunsmith. "How can I ever thank you, Clint?"

When he looked into her beautiful face, a glow of gratitude and admiration lit up her features and Clint knew how he'd like her to thank him.

"You just did, ma'am," was all he said.

ELEVEN

Bruno dragged Jimmy Markham across the threshold. A black porter, dressed in railroad overalls and cap, watched with dismay and fearfully clutched his bucket and mop. He was about to advise Clint Adams to put some clothes on, but the pistol in the Gunsmith's hand discouraged the porter.

"Maybe I should clean up later, suhs," the man remarked woodenly.

"Wait a minute," Stansfield Lloyd snapped. "Give me that bucket."

"Suh?"

Lloyd pitched the dirty water from the bucket into Markham's face. The youth coughed violently and rolled on his stomach to throw up. Lloyd kicked him sharply in the ribs.

"Get up, you jackass!" the gunman ordered.

Markham stared up at Lloyd. "Stan, I—"

"I've got one thing to say to you, kid," Clint announced in a cold, flat voice. "If you ever touch that girl again, you'd better know how to do more with a gun than twirl it on your finger."

"You won't have to do nothin', Adams," Lloyd growled. He glared at Markham. "What's wrong with you? Manhandling the boss's daughter like she was a saloon whore!"

46

"She's a good-lookin' woman, Stan," Markham replied feebly as he rose unsteadily to his feet. "And it sure looked like she wanted it."

"That's why she screamed, huh?" Lloyd hissed.

The pistolman's arm became a blur and suddenly the muzzle of his Remington .44 was jammed under Markham's chin and the hammer had been cocked back. The youth stiffened in terror and closed his eyes as if to eliminate the danger by not seeing it. *Lloyd's fast,* Clint noted. *Very fast.*

"I usually grant a feller one mistake, Jimmy," Lloyd whispered, his tone a soft howling wind in a graveyard. "You made a real big one and you'd better not make another. Understand?"

Markham tried to nod, but the gun barrel in the hollow of his jaw arrested the movement. "I understand, Stan," he replied through clenched teeth. "I won't do nothin' like it again."

"What's going on here?" the voice of Walter Patterson demanded.

The Pinkerton detective waddled through the corridor, red-faced and panting from unaccustomed exertion. Lloyd shrugged. "Just a little misunderstanding," the gunman replied.

Patterson glanced at the faces of the escort team and thrust a finger at Markham. "What happened to him?"

"Got into an argument that sorta got outta hand," Lloyd answered. "It's over now."

"I was told a woman screamed back here."

"That was Miss Mather," Lloyd nodded. "She thought she saw an injun at her window. Just a bad dream. Wanta ask her about it?"

"I told you men that I expected trouble from you and I see I wasn't mistaken," Patterson declared. "I will not tolerate this sort of conduct on my train."

"*Your* train?" Bruno chuckled. "Ain't that something?"

"Does the railroad know you own this rig?" Vargas inquired with a wiry grin.

The Pinkerton man thrust his fists into his wide hips. "If there's another incident by *any* of you, I shall have all five of you put off this train. Is that clear?"

"None of us is deaf," Lloyd answered with a thin smile. "Don't worry, feller."

Patterson turned to Clint Adams. "And what is your excuse for running around in your underwear, mister?"

"It was all I had on when I heard the lady scream," the Gunsmith replied. He raised the revolver. "But I dressed for the occasion."

Before the Pinkerton could voice a response, Clint headed back to his quarters. Entering the compartment, he peered out the window. The bleak Texas desert shuffled by. Cactus, rocks and mesquite amid oceans of sand. Barren, primitive land that seemed incapable of sustaining life. Yet lizards, snakes, birds and scorpions thrived here—not to mention the Apache. Nomads, the Apache were Indians of the plains and deserts who seldom put down roots for long. Their way of life was savage and harsh by the standards of most other Indian tribes as well as the white man's. It had made them a clever, cunning and cruel people. The train was traveling deeper into the heart of Apache territory.

The only thing worse than being stranded out here alone, Clint thought, *would be getting stranded with four cutthroats like Lloyd, Vargas, Bruno and Markham. . . .*

TWELVE

The Gunsmith spent the next six hours getting familiar with the train. If Apache or *bandidos* decided to attack, Clint wanted every edge he could get and knowing the battleground better than the enemy is one of the best advantages one can have.

Clint attracted some curious stares from the passengers as he marched through the aisles. No one asked what he was doing or why he carried a Springfield carbine canted on his shoulder. Many looked away when he drew closer. Everybody had clearly heard about Linda Mather's escort team and wanted nothing to do with them.

The Gunsmith didn't like being categorized with the other four men. Vargas had two lumps of hate instead of a brain and a heart, and Markham was a vicious young rattlesnake. Bruno seemed to be a nasty brute, but Clint guessed the big man's bald head wasn't empty since he'd displayed better self-control than either Vargas or Markham—which might make him all the more dangerous. Then there was Lloyd, the cold-blooded, lightning-fast killing machine, probably the worst of the lot.

Great company I'm keeping these days, the Gunsmith thought. *No wonder these folks think I'm a mad dog that walks on its hind legs*.

Clint Adams relieved Mike Vargas of guard duty at

one o'clock in the morning. Stationed at Linda's door, the surly cross-breed held a Winchester rifle in addition to his gunbelt and ever-present knife.

"Ready to get some sleep?" Clint inquired.

"*Sí*," Vargas confirmed. "*Yo soy fatigado*. You know what to do, no? Just stand here and guard the door."

"Sure," Clint nodded. "No sweat."

"You'd better take this job serious, Adams," Stansfield Lloyd growled as he approached the pair.

"A couple things I take real serious include earning money and traveling through Apache territory," the Gunsmith assured him.

"You full awake?" the gunman demanded.

"Would you fetch me a cup of coffee if I wasn't?" Clint asked. "I told you I take Apaches seriously. Even when I sleep I'm half awake. Don't worry about me, all right?"

"Ain't *you* I'm worried about," Lloyd snarled. "Come with me, Mike. I wanta talk to you."

"*Christo*," Vargas cursed. "Can't it wait until morning?"

"It's already morning and it can't wait," the gunman replied gruffly.

Clint watched the pair depart, happy to be rid of them. He placed his Springfield in a corner. Clint seldom used a long gun, favoring his pistol, but if the train was suddenly surrounded by attacking Apaches on horseback, the extra range of the rifle could be more than welcome. However, if an attack occurred in the narrow corridor in front of Linda's door, the modified double-action Colt would be a more practical weapon for fast, close quarters combat shooting.

The Gunsmith mentally prepared himself to cope with six hours of boredom. At least, he hoped it would be boring. Only a lunatic would prefer an invasion by kill-crazy savages to a few quiet hours. As time crept by, however, Clint considered his current task with apprehension. Something about the whole business seemed false, but he couldn't put his figurative finger on it. The others knew something he didn't and he suspected this ignorance might well cost him his life if he wasn't very careful. . . .

The dull click of metal startled the Gunsmith; reacting to the unexpected sound before he realized it was the doorknob to Linda's room, Clint reached for his holstered .45 Colt. The brass bulb turned and the door opened. Linda Mather's lovely face appeared in the gap. Clint's hand fell away from the butt of his revolver.

"I thought you'd be on duty now," she smiled. "That's a comfort."

"Glad you feel that way, ma'am," the Gunsmith replied. "Is there something I can do for you?"

"First thing is you can stop calling me *ma'am* or *Miss Mather*. My name is Linda."

"What else can I do for you, Linda?"

"Maybe we can do something for each other," she suggested. The door creaked open in invitation. "Come in."

Clint glanced down the corridor. "I'm supposed to be standing guard out here."

"You're protecting me, right?" Linda smiled. "You can do that inside my room just as well as you can in the hallway."

The Gunsmith shrugged, gathered up his Springfield and stepped across the threshold. "If Lloyd checks on me, I hope you'll be willing to explain things, Linda."

She laughed lightly. "Don't tell me you're afraid of Stan, Clint."

"I'm not afraid of him," Clint answered. "I just don't

like the idea of having to kill a man because of a misunderstanding."

"Oh?" Linda raised an eyebrow. "Are you so sure you can take Stan? I've heard about your reputation with a gun. They say you can draw and fire before the other man can even get his gun out of the holster. Is that true?"

"It's happened," Clint replied. He didn't tell her that, in fact, only one man had ever managed to clear leather before Clint shot him.

"Well, you don't have to worry about Stan for a while," Linda assured him. "He's a creature of habit. Regular as clockwork, he's been checking on the guards every three hours. You won't need to pit your skill against his."

"That's nice," Clint remarked as he glanced about the room. Earlier, he'd been too busy thrashing Markham to pay much attention to the decor. Twice the size of a normal sleeper, Linda's room was a luxury compartment with a carpeted floor, fine furniture and velvet curtains in the windows. Pink cherubim were painted on the tinplated ceiling that reflected light from the kerosine lamp mounted on a wall. Satin sheets covered the wide mattress of a brass-framed bed, and a cream-colored chest of drawers added to the elegance of the room. A small circular table and two chairs completed the furnishings.

Linda's luggage, three large steamer trunks, filled one side of the room. Two of them sat on end and stood open to serve as closets for the lady; expensive clothing of silk and lace hung inside. The third lay flat on the floor, its heavy lid secured by a padlock.

"You seem a little nervous, Clint," she remarked, closing the door. "If Stan doesn't frighten you, certainly *I* shouldn't."

"You're a beautiful woman," Clint stated. "That makes you as potentially dangerous as any man with a gun or a knife."

"Oh!" Linda exclaimed with delight. "You're thinking that perhaps I invited Jimmy Markham into my room like this, teased him, and when he made advances, I started to scream just to start trouble. Is that it?"

"Some women think that sort of thing is a lot of fun," the Gunsmith answered.

"Jimmy is a boy," Linda remarked. "I want a man. That little nuisance has had his lustful eye on me ever since Daddy hired him three days ago. Apparently he thought I might surrender to his boorish charm once we were alone."

"Your daddy hired him three days ago?" Clint smiled thinly. "Is that when he got the other three too?"

"I guess so. . . ." Linda looked at him with curiosity, almost apprehension. "Why do you ask?"

"Those four aren't strangers to each other," Clint stated. "They call each other by first name and none of them are exactly the gregarious type. Markham and Vargas were willing to bet on Bruno in a bare-knuckle fight with two men. That means they must know him pretty well to figure he could win. When we heard the commotion, Lloyd *and* your father guessed what was happening. Those four have worked together in the past . . . and I think your daddy knows it."

"You're right," the girl agreed. "Lloyd said he had some highly competent friends and Daddy agreed to take them on the payroll. As for him knowing about Bruno's prowess as a pugilist, the brute fought a couple of our ranch hands in a similar contest to prove his ability."

"Does he plan to punch Apache arrows out of the air if we're attacked?" Clint inquired dryly.

"I imagine he knows how to use a gun as well as his fists," Linda sighed. "Daddy did the hiring, not me."

"I'm not terribly impressed with his choice of men."

"He hired *you,* didn't he?"

"Yeah," Clint admitted. "Almost makes me wonder about myself."

"You're different from the others," Linda commented. "That's why I'm attracted to you."

Clint allowed his gaze to travel from her lovely features to the shapely body beneath. Clad only in a thin pink nightgown, the curves of her figure were handsomely displayed by the lamplight. The neckline was low enough to reveal the tops of her large, firm breasts, and the hem reached to the middle of her calves, hinting at the shape of her long legs.

"The feeling's mutual, lady," he assured her.

The girl put her hands on the straps of her garment and slipped them from her shoulders; the gown fell to her feet. The promise of naked beauty had not been false. Her full breasts swelled like sweet, ripe melons. The slender belly flared into wide hips, but her thighs and legs were tapered and smooth. Her dark reddish-brown triangle mutely invited the Gunsmith to satisfy the longing he felt in his own loins.

Clint quickly removed his own clothing. Linda appraised his physique with equal appreciation. Without uttering a word, Clint stepped forward and took the woman in his arms. They kissed hard, lips crushing together, tongues probing the caverns of their mouths. Their hands caressed and fondled passionately, feeling each other's willing flesh.

The Gunsmith picked her up and carried her to the bed. Linda lay on her back, legs spread in invitation. However, Clint took his time, skillfully stroking her taut, willing body and kissing her breasts and neck. His tongue and teeth gently teased her nipples until they stood as hard and erect as his own manhood. Deft fingers moved along her thighs, finding the crevice between them, stimulating her with his touch.

"Oh, God!" Linda moaned. "I want you in me, Clint! I want you right now!"

The Gunsmith mounted her, his member swollen to full length. Stiff and eager, his maleness found her love triangle as he lowered himself onto his elbows. Clint churned his hips slowly, working himself deeper into the girl. Linda groaned with pleasure as he began to pump back and forth. He felt her rise to meet his lunges and increased his motion—faster, harder, deeper.

Her nails raked his back in passion and her cries of joy nearly turned to shouts before he clamped his mouth over hers. Clint's tongue joined the rhythm of his thrusts as he rode Linda to her limit.

Then her body convulsed as an orgasm overcame her. Clint worked her to the peak of her endurance a second time. Only then did he release himself as Linda squealed with delight, wrapping her arms and legs around him to savor the throbbing hardness within. Then they lay still, breathing hard and coated by a film of perspiration.

"Oh, Clint," she whispered. "That was wonderful."

"Was?" he replied softly, kissing her earlobe. "We haven't finished yet."

THIRTEEN

Walter Patterson wearily consulted his copper-plated pocket watch and frowned when he saw what time it was. Past two o'clock. Waddling through the aisles of a passenger car, he barely glanced at the empty seats. They resembled the pews of a church between congregations. The ungrateful louts on the train didn't appreciate the service he supplied—namely, protection against outlaws, hostile Indians or possibly those five hardcases who rode at the rear of the locomotive.

Those bastards were supposed to be guarding the daughter of some rich rancher or banker, but the Pinkerton man knew better. No self-respecting businessman would hire a group of ruffians like those five. No, they were up to no good, although Patterson had yet to find out what sort of mischief was afoot. Well, he'd worry about that later. It was time to get some sleep.

He stepped onto a terrace between two cars. The roar of the steam engine assaulted his ears and he grimaced at the stench of soot and coal dust. How could those engineers tolerate such filth and noise? They must be stupid enough to enjoy it, he decided as he prepared to cross over to the next car.

"*Buenas noches,*" a voice whispered.

Patterson turned suddenly, startled to discover one of the ruffians, the Mexican or whatever he was, standing on the terrace beside him.

"What—" the detective began, fighting to control his racing heart, "what do you want?"

"I just wanted to say *adiós*, fat one," Vargas smiled.

A bolt of steel flickered in his right fist. Patterson's mouth opened, but the assassin's other hand fell upon it to stifle his cry. The Pinkerton man tried to reach for his holstered Hopkins & Allen revolver. Vargas was faster. The dagger sank into the detective's paunch. Vargas twisted his wrist, turning the blade to increase the size of the wound. Patterson trembled in agony as Vargas pulled the knife free and stabbed him twice more, once in the chest and a third time between the ribs.

"*Vaya con El Diablo,*" the killer chuckled, shoving the corpse over the side. Walter Patterson's body struck the ground like a side of beef and rolled across the desert sand. "Go with the devil."

FOURTEEN

The next few days passed without much excitement. The escort team took turns guarding Linda Mather's quarters; Clint handled his share of the duty and prowled the train or slept when possible. Every night, he accepted an invitation to share Linda's bed. She proved to be an expert lover, if less than generous; she seemed driven by her lust and though Clint found her an intriguing bedmate, her basic coldness limited his pleasure. Clint wasn't looking for everlasting love, but he liked his women to have heart. Still, he was glad to have the diversion from the rest of the company.

The Gunsmith's distrust of his traveling companions increased with each passing day. He was especially leery of Jimmy Markham, who might decide to repay him for the beating he'd received. Clint slept while Vargas stood guard duty, aware of the man's hatred for Anglos and his habit of guzzling liquor every night, thus limiting any opportunity for the knife artist to catch him off guard while he lay flat on his back. He never left his quarters without his guns, generally taking the Springfield as well as the ever-present .45 Colt on his hip and the .22 New Line tucked in his belt and hidden under his shirt.

Most of the time, Clint prowled the train and checked on his wagon and gear in the cattle car. He was distressed when he discovered the ordeal the trip had placed on Duke and his two team horses. Clint hadn't realized the miserable conditions the beasts would be forced to endure in the cattle car. Close to the engine, the compartment was constantly bombarded by soot and smoke. Duke's beautiful coat was always covered with black residue and his nostrils were often plugged with grime.

Clint brushed the gelding's coat every chance he got and whenever the train stopped for a prolonged period of time, he gave Duke some fresh air and exercise. While the train received water or coal at remote railroad stations Clint mounted his horse and rode laps around the area to let the poor beast stretch his legs.

"Never again, big fella," he promised Duke, hoping that somehow the animal would understand his words. "Never again."

When he wasn't tending to his horses, checking his gear or servicing Linda, the Gunsmith read whatever he could get his hands on—old newspapers, dime novels and a King James Bible he borrowed from Reverend Kluger. The gaunt minister had been startled when Clint asked if he had a spare Bible and woodenly agreed to loan it to the "gunman."

"I hope you find guidance in the Good Book, young man," Kluger commented.

"Thanks," Clint replied. "I could sure use some."

The train stopped at El Paso to deliver and pick up cargo. The railroad made most of its profit in freight and seemed more concerned with it than the people on board. Several passengers got off at the small Texas border town and a dozen Mexicans climbed on to replace them. The conductor paid little attention to the new arrivals after making certain their tickets were in order, but Stansfield Lloyd, Vargas and Jimmy Markham observed the passengers with cold suspicion.

The Mexicans were divided into three separate groups. Eight *peónes,* clad in white cotton shirts and trousers, straw sombreros and leather sandles, formed the largest party. Their heads were bowed low as they mounted the iron steps of a boxcar, carrying small cloth handbags.

Two young *vaqueros,* dressed in colorful silk shirts, vests, chaps and fancy spurs, also climbed on board. Both men wore ornate gunbelts and one carried a guitar.

The third group consisted only of two women. One was a short, thickly built lady in her forties with a wide homely face. The other, taller and thinner, walked with the proud, arrogant stride of an aristocrat. She was lovely, with large dark eyes, high cheekbones and the straight nose of a Creole. Her glossy raven-black hair was bound to the top of her head by a silver clasp to form a sort of crown. The young woman wore an elegant black lace dress that accented her long, lean figure.

"Looky there," Markham remarked. "Ain't she a fancy little filly?"

"*Sí,*" Vargas muttered sourly. "She's a *rica,* probably the daughter of a *ranchero* or a *politico.* The old woman with her is a chaperon. It is a custom for such fine ladies of good families in *Mejico* to travel in such a manner."

"She's mighty purty," Markham stated.

"If you said hello to her, she'd spit in your face," Vargas informed him. "Her kind don't associate with the lower classes."

"Figure those other greasers are with her?" Lloyd inquired. Clint was surprised by the gunman's use of such an ethnic slur in front of Vargas, but then realized the question had been directed to the cross-breed. "Maybe the *peónes* are her servants and Daddy sent along the other two Mexs to protect her."

Vargas shook his head. "The porters carried her luggage, not the *peónes,* so they don't work for her. I saw one of the *vaqueros* tip his hat at her and she didn't even acknowledge him. No, they do not travel together."

"Keep an eye on 'em," Lloyd instructed. "Especially those two wearing guns."

"Reckon they might be trouble?" Markham asked, flexing his fingers over the butts of his holstered Colts.

"No sense takin' chances," the pistolman replied.

The Gunsmith frowned. The trio seemed too suspicious of the newcomers to merit simple caution. Again, Clint felt there was more to the escort mission than he'd been told. He considered returning the fifteen hundred dollars he'd received in advance and quitting right then and there. El Paso was as good a place as any for a traveling gunsmith to unload his wagon and start looking for business.

Yet, he'd be virtually penniless in a small border town, a prospect that didn't appeal to him, and they'd already completed half the journey to Yuma. Once again, he rejected the warnings of his instincts and elected to see the job through to the end.

FIFTEEN

The train continued to roll on into the New Mexico Territory. The surroundings changed dramatically with multi-colored rock formations and patches of vegetation with bright flowers a startling contrast to the drab gray and sandy tan deserts of Texas. Purple, black and gold filled the arid region as if God has splashed a rainbow across the stony monuments and rock walls. Even the sand varied in shades from dark brown to light yellow.

Mesquite, barrel cactus and cottonwood trees dotted the terrain. Occasionally, a roadrunner or collar lizard appeared, dashing on its hind legs in an oddly human manner as if to remind man that he isn't as different from other animals as he likes to think.

Clint Adams continued to roam the train between guard watches, observing the new passengers. The *peónes* remained close together, quiet and seemingly spellbound by their trip on the great *caballo de hierro*. By contrast, the *vaqueros* appeared pleased with the journey and killed time by singing Spanish ballads to the music of the guitarist cowboy. They smiled at Clint and nodded greetings when he shuffled by.

"*Señor,*" the guitar player said, "why do you walk back and forth with that gun on your shoulder? Do you expect trouble from *los indios*?"

"If that happens, señor," the other *vaquero* declared,

"you can rely on Roberto and I to help you fight them."

"Thanks," the Gunsmith nodded, hoping the pair were exactly what they appeared to be, a couple of Mexican cowpunchers heading north of the border in search of employment on an Anglo ranch—and not a pair of wolves in *vaquero* clothing.

The two female passengers occasionally glanced up at Clint with distaste, but neither spoke to him or acknowledged his presence. He decided to reserve judgment about the new arrivals for the time being. The Gunsmith wondered why he hadn't seen the Pinkerton since he'd warned the escort team about their behavior at the beginning of the journey. Then again, who wanted to see that jackass anyway?

The following afternoon, Clint encountered Linda and Stansfield Lloyd in the dining car eating lunch. She gestured for him to join them. The gunfighter scowled, but he didn't voice any objection when Clint sat down beside the girl.

"Decided not to dine in your room today, Miss Mather?" Clint remarked.

"I'm getting cabin fever in there," she answered. "Have you eaten?"

"I had a big breakfast," the Gunsmith said. "So I'm not going to eat lunch. Too much food in a man's stomach isn't good if he has to move fast."

"It's not good for a girl's figure either," Linda commented, pushing her plate aside. Only half the meal had been consumed.

"Well, Adams," Lloyd said, rolling a cigarette. "Looks like you're gonna collect an easy three thousand dollars, don't it?"

"I hope so," Clint admitted. "But we haven't reached Yuma yet."

"Let's worry about that later," Linda urged.

"It's our job to worry about trouble," Lloyd stated.

"Worrying about things never helps," the Gunsmith remarked. "We can just try to prepare for trouble and handle it the best we can when and if it comes along."

"Business again!" the girl rolled her eyes with exasperation. She pushed back her chair and rose. Clint, always a gentleman, was immediately on his feet. "Would you please see me to my door?" she asked him.

"My pleasure, ma'am," the Gunsmith nodded.

He felt the pistolman's icy gaze at the base of his neck as he escorted Linda from the dining car. The girl's arm slipped around the biceps of his left arm.

"You ever get a yearning in the afternoon?" she whispered.

"Do you think this is a wise idea?" Clint asked.

"Don't worry about Stan," Linda smiled. "I know how to handle him."

"Is that so?" Clint inquired dryly. He noticed the two Mexican women seated at another table. The younger lady was watching them with such intensity that frost seemed to form on the hairs at the back of Clint's neck.

"Of course," Linda assured him.

"What about your man in Yuma?"

"If I couldn't handle him"—she grinned impishly—"we wouldn't be getting married."

Bruno raised his meager eyebrows with surprise when he saw the couple approach. The big man stood sentry in front of the girl's room, armed only with his S&W revolver and a lot of muscle. Linda opened the door and entered. The Gunsmith began to follow, but a steel-taloned hand grabbed his arm.

"Where do you think you're going, Adams?" Bruno demanded, his small dark eyes narrowed into hot razor slits in his egglike face.

"He's paying me a visit," Linda answered curtly. "Any objections?"

"Not from me," the brute smiled thinly. "Maybe from others."

"My problem," she said stiffly.

"Yeah," Bruno released Clint. "Your problem . . . and yours too, Adams."

The Gunsmith entered the girl's quarters and closed the door. He flexed his arm to circulate blood into the limb. Bruno had a grip like a beartrap.

"What was that about?" he asked Linda.

"He probably thinks word will get back to my father or to David, my fiancé in Yuma, about our conduct."

"Could be he's right," Clint commented.

"I can handle them," the girl crooned. "Don't worry."

"I'm not worried"—he shrugged—"about *you*."

SIXTEEN

Linda Mather didn't waste any time. She immediately stripped off her clothing and headed for the bed. Clint followed her example, taking care to hide his .22 New Line Colt from view by sticking it into a boot before dropping his shirt over the footgear. He didn't want the girl to know about his belly gun because he didn't trust her any more than he did the rest of his traveling companions.

Clint draped his gunbelt over the headboard in his customary manner and stepped out of his trousers. To his surprise, he saw Linda poised on the mattress on her hands and knees.

"Figure it's about time for a little variety," she commented coyly. "Hop on board and we'll go for a ride."

Linda had become increasingly more crude in her lovemaking; the Gunsmith, however, never failed to try to please a lady, so he climbed into the bed, placing his knees between her legs.

His hands slowly caressed her smooth firm buttocks, the backs of her thighs, and the sides of her calves. Then his fingers moved deftly between her thighs, stroking and probing with assurance. Linda rocked her body to and fro to receive his touch.

"Oh, Jesus, Clint!" she moaned. "You sure know how to get a girl ready!"

Clint's penis, now erect and hard, soon took his hand's place and Linda hummed with pleasure as he worked himself slowly into her. Soon she was gripping him like an internal fist, her body jerking back and forth quickly.

Clint rammed himself deeply into Linda's hot flesh. The slap of her buttocks against his lower abdomen filled the room with subdued applause, gradually becoming louder and more rapid, accompanied by the passionate, labored breathing of the couple. Suddenly Linda gasped and trembled with her orgasm.

Clint continued to ride her to the heights of a second pleasure journey, his maleness straining to bring her satisfaction, teeth clenched in the effort to hold back until she could join him. When Linda's flesh convulsed in another spasm of ecstasy, Clint gratefully released his seed within her, his own fulfillment achieved at last.

Then a man's scream penetrated the door and the sound of a fierce brawl commanded the Gunsmith's full and immediate attention. Linda squealed when he abruptly withdrew and bounded from the bed, snatching his Colt .45 from its holster at the headboard. He managed to gather up his trousers as he charged for the door.

Opening it a crack, he saw two of the *peón* passengers sprawled on the floor of the corridor. The other six were gathered around Bruno, knives flashing at the brute. The big man's fists, forearms and feet lashed out. thudding into flesh and knocking aside opponents. Bruno was holding his own remarkably well considering the odds. He seemed to ignore the slashing blades as he fought bare-handed against the group. However, the *peónes'* superior numbers and sharp-steel advantage would soon be too much even for Bruno.

One man stepped behind the muscle-bound defender

and prepared to lunge a knife into Bruno's kidney. Clint couldn't shoot the *peón* because the bullet would be apt to punch right through him into Bruno. The Gunsmith closed in rapidly, raised his gun arm and brought the butt of his revolver down on the base of the aggressor's neck. Bone cracked and the Mexican collapsed with a broken neck.

Another knife-wielding opponent charged Clint from the side. The Gunsmith whirled and shot him in the face. The assassin's corpse smacked into a wall and slid to the floor as two more Mexican killers jumped away from Bruno and raised their loose cotton shirts and tried to draw revolvers that were hidden under the garments.

Clint's double-action Colt snarled in response, firing a round into each man's chest before either could bring his weapon into play. One man's body crashed to the floor, but the other jerked forward from the impact of a .44 bullet between the shoulder blades fired by Stansfield Lloyd, who had just appeared at the mouth of the corridor.

Both the pistolman and Mike Vargas had been attracted by the scream that had alerted the Gunsmith to the carnage. Lloyd's Remington swung toward another *peón* and fired a round into the man's abdomen. The would-be assassin doubled up and Lloyd put another slug through the man's straw sombrero and into the top of his skull.

A fifth Mexican managed to produce an old .36 caliber cap-and-ball Navy Colt with a cut-down barrel. Both Clint's Colt and Lloyd's Remington roared in unison. Lloyd shot the man squarely in the heart, and the Gunsmith's .45 bullet blasted its way into the *peón's* left temple making a gory exit via the other side of his head.

Only one Mexican invader remained on his feet. He

held his empty hands high in surrender. Vargas kicked a knife across the floor toward the man.

"*Coge el cuchillo, bastardo!*" Vargas demanded, stepping forward and holstering his six-gun.

When the cross-breed dragged his ivory-handled dagger from its sheath, the *peón* realized why Vargas had told him to pick up the knife. Aware he would die one way or the other, his *machismo* rose to the challenge.

Vargas smiled as the man stooped and gathered up the knife. The dagger flashed and the Mexican jumped out of range, but Vargas suddenly dropped to one knee and slashed the retreating man's inner thigh.

"That's enough, Vargas!" Clint shouted.

The knife artist ignored him. "Next time I cut his *huevos* off," Vargas chuckled.

With a cry of rage, the *peón* attacked, lashing out with his knife. Vargas danced away from the blade. Quickly he tossed the dagger from his right hand to his left and lunged forward. The Mexican screamed as the point of Vargas's weapon bit into his side to slide between two ribs and pierce a lung. Vargas seized his opponent and pulled him to the floor. The dagger rose in an overhand grip and then fell twice as Vargas stabbed the man in the chest.

Clint heard one of the *peónes* moan and turned to see Bruno knelt beside a man who was about to regain consciousness. The big man grabbed the Mexican's head, one huge hand gripping the top of his skull while the other held him under the jaw, and twisted it forcibly. The ugly crunch of vertebrae filled the corridor.

"You didn't have to kill those two," the Gunsmith declared, glancing down at the eight bodies that littered the floor.

"How come you ain't got nothing on, Adams?" Lloyd demanded, staring at Clint's nakedness.

The Gunsmith was too angry to be embarrassed, but he pulled on his trousers as he spoke. "We could have questioned these men. Maybe we could have found out why the hell they attacked us."

"These *peónes* must have figured there was something worth stealing in Linda's room 'cause we had a guard on it," Vargas suggested.

"These men weren't *peónes*," Clint replied. "How many Mexican peasants can afford guns or ammunition? Look at their feet. A *peón's* feet are calloused and dark brown from exposure to the sun. These men have been wearing boots most of the time and probably riding more than walking from the looks of the soles of their feet."

"Christ," Bruno muttered, examining a minor cut on his forearm. "I would have been cut to ribbons if'n Adams hadn't been around."

"Yeah," Lloyd said tensely. "And it's pretty obvious what he was doin' in Miss Mather's room too."

The pistolman faced Clint, his Remington still in hand. The Gunsmith's Colt was also held ready. Both men's weapons pointed at the floor. Clint recognized the killer-lust in Lloyd's eyes. The gunman wanted to shoot him down, but he was a professional and realized his anger would be apt to make him careless. After a couple of long, tense seconds, Lloyd holstered his revolver.

"You keep away from her, Adams," Lloyd hissed.

"*Uno momento,*" Vargas said. "Where's Jimmy?"

"It's too early for him to be drunk," Bruno remarked. "You'd think a gunshot would have brought him galloping this way to join the party."

"Check his quarters, Mike," Lloyd ordered. "Bruno, you feel fit enough to stand guard?"

"Sure," the big man turned to Clint. "I'm beholdin' to you, feller."

"Adam was saving his own hide," Lloyd spat. "You don't owe him nothin'!"

"Working with you guys is more fun than going to a dentist who uses rusty pliers," Clint muttered as he headed for Linda's room to get the rest of his clothes.

A conductor—the name on his breast pocket was *Andrew Waitley*—cautiously appeared at the mouth of the corridor. "What's going on here?" the emaciated, middle-aged man inquired fearfully, gazing down at the corpse-littered floor in horror.

"A square dance sort of got out of hand," Clint snorted.

Suddenly, a distraught Vargas nearly ran into Waitley as he charged back into the hallway. "Stan, you better come with me. Pronto!"

"Why?" Lloyd replied. "Is something wrong?"

"I found Jimmy lyin' on his bunk—dead!" Vargas answered. "Somebody stabbed him to death."

"What's wrong with that?" the Gunsmith shrugged.

SEVENTEEN

Despite his callous remark, Clint hastily donned his clothing and soon joined Stansfield Lloyd, Mike Vargas, Andrew Waitley and a pair of horrified passengers at the open door of the compartment Jimmy Markham and Bruno had shared. Lloyd and Vargas stepped across the threshold and examined the lifeless lump sprawled across the blood-splattered bunk.

Jimmy Markham's corpse was stark naked, lying on his side, glassy eyes open in amazement and horror. The boy's mouth hung open, the tongue curled back. Clawed fingers still clung to the scarlet-streaked sheets.

"He was lying on his belly when I found him," Vargas explained. "I figured he was dead, but I sorta turned him over to check for a heartbeat."

Clint moved forward and placed a hand on Markham's shoulder. The flesh was still warm, but beginning to cool and stiffen. He pulled the corpse forward, rolling it face first on the mattress. A still-damp stain surrounded a deep slit between his shoulder blades. Two similar wounds were located at the small of his back.

"Stabbed in the spine," the Gunsmith declared in a clinical manner. "That would have paralyzed him even if it didn't kill him. Stabbed in both kidneys too."

"Didn't take no chances, huh?" Lloyd remarked.

"The wounds look like a double-edged blade was used," Clint added. "Probably a dagger similar to yours, Vargas."

The knife artist glared at him. "You tryin' to say you think I did it?"

"If I thought that I wouldn't say anything in front of you, Vargas," Clint told him. "I'm just telling you what I see."

"Calm down, Mike," Lloyd urged. "Adams ain't accusing you of anything. Those greasers must've seen Jimmy go into the sleeper alone and killed him.

"Why'd they take his clothes off?" the conductor asked. His face looked as though he'd been eating cold ashes.

"Maybe they tortured him to get information about—" Vargas began. "About something."

Clint found Markham's clothes on the floor by the bunk. He picked up a shirt. "The cloth isn't ripped," he remarked. "And the only marks on the kid's body are the stab wounds that killed him."

"Probably made Jimmy strip and threatened to torture him," Lloyd suggested. "He panicked and they stuck him to shut him up."

"Maybe," Clint allowed. "The mattress is indented too deeply for only one person to have been on it."

"Shit," Vargas snorted. "You tryin' to play detective, Adams?"

"Don't you know about the Gunsmith, here?" Lloyd asked in a mocking tone. "He used to be a lawman. Did it for almost twenty years way I heard it. That right, Adams?"

"Eighteen years," Clint admitted.

"Is it true you knew old Wild Bill before his luck ran out?"

"Yeah," Clint said stiffly. Bill Hickok had been the

Gunsmith's closest friend for many years. Hickok's recent death had been very hard for Clint to deal with, although he'd known Bill's days were numbered ever since he'd served as Hickok's deputy in Abilene back in 1871. Bill's eyesight had been failing him and he'd taken to drinking too much. The Gunsmith himself had crawled into a bottle after Hickok's death, where he would have stayed if he hadn't been brought out of his drunken stupor to ride off in quest of justice—or revenge. Clint would have settled for either at the time.

"You reckon you coulda taken Hickok, Adams?" Lloyd inquired.

"Bill was faster than God," the Gunsmith replied, sadly shaking his head.

"Speaking of detectives," Waitley commented, "I'd better tell Mr. Patterson about this terrible incident."

"Ain't as bad as it could have been," Lloyd declared. "All them sneaky Mex killers is dead now."

"Oh, my!" the conductor began in a stunned voice. "What will we do with the bodies?"

"It's sort of a custom to bury dead people," Clint mused dryly.

"Oh, of course," Waitley nodded woodenly. "We'll have to stop the train and see to them."

"We'll bury Jimmy," Lloyd answered. "But the coyotes and buzzards can help themselves to the other bastards."

"We'll help," the Gunsmith announced. "At least, I will."

Vargas looked at him with surprise. "Why should we bother, Adams?"

"Somebody has to bury them," Clint replied. "Only right we lend a hand. After all, we killed them."

Impromptu funeral services were held and the train continued on, leaving nine unmarked graves by the side of the tracks. Scavengers would later invade the mounds. Desert winds would scatter the sand, and the bones, dried under the merciless sun, would eventually turn to dust. Within two years, there'd be no trace of the dead men or their graves.

However, burial rituals are for the living, Clint figured, to soothe the grief-stricken, or as in this case, to satisfy a desire for civilized behavior following savage death.

The guard shifts for Clint, Vargas and Bruno were extended to eight hours to compensate for the loss of Jimmy Markham. The Gunsmith relieved Mike Vargas at midnight and assumed his station by Linda's door. The knife artist didn't utter a word as he carried his rifle under an arm and walked from the corridor.

Clint watched Vargas depart. Any doubts he may have had about the deadly abilities of his traveling companions had dissolved after seeing them in action during the battle with the so-called *peónes*. Unfortunately, nothing had happened to dispel any of his suspicions or answer any of his questions.

Linda's door opened. He turned to see the girl at the threshold, a coy smile on her lovely face. "Our plans for this afternoon were cut sort of short," she purred. "Why don't we make up for it now?"

"Why don't you explain a couple things first?" he replied flatly.

"What sort of things?" Linda frowned.

"Those men purposely tried to raid your quarters," Clint stated. "Why?"

"They must have assumed there was something valuable in here," she shrugged, repeating the same excuse Vargas had made earlier. "I understand the poor classes in Mexico can get pretty desperate."

Clint noticed Linda's right hand slowly massaged her

ribcage. He couldn't see through the nightgown, but he guessed she had a bruise there. "What happened to you?"

"I fell against the table when the train stopped," Linda shrugged again. "It's nothing."

"Those men weren't *peónes*," Clint insisted, returning to the original topic. "And I think you know it."

"You don't sound like you're in a very loving mood, Clint," she remarked stiffly.

"I'm damn tired of getting half-truths and downright lies," he said sharply. "My life is on the line and I really haven't been told why."

"Well"—the girl glared at him—"if that's the way you want to act, you can just stand out there and look at the goddamn walls all night!"

Linda slammed the door hard.

The Gunsmith glanced around the corridor. "Hello, walls," he sighed.

EIGHTEEN

Wearily, the Gunsmith consulted his turnip-shaped pocket watch to discover it was almost four o'clock in the morning. He regretted his conversation with Linda Mather, not only because it terminated their sexual pleasures, but because it hadn't done a damn thing to solve any of the mysteries about the journey that continued to prey on his mind.

However, it had contributed to two suspicions. Unless Linda was just plain dumb, which Clint didn't believe, she had decided to agree with the theory about the attempted *peón* raid although she probably realized it was absurd. This meant she had a closer association with Lloyd, Vargas and Bruno then she'd implied. Especially Lloyd. Clint had recognized the pistolman's anger when he'd discovered the Gunsmith had been stark naked in Linda's room. Lloyd had felt more than mere resentment. He'd been excessively jealous, almost to the level of killing in blind anger, something totally contrary to the nature of a cold-blooded professional like Stansfield Lloyd.

The Gunsmith guessed that Linda's bruised ribs had been acquired from a punch by Lloyd delivered sometime between the funeral services and when Clint assumed guard duty. The gunman hadn't hit her in the face because a bruise there would be too obvious. Why

77

had she lied? Because she was afraid of Lloyd? Quite possible. Could she be trying to protect Clint from Lloyd? Not likely. In fact it could even be the other way around. Just what the hell was going on anyway?

Suddenly Clint was hurled off balance. He slammed into a wall, barely turning a shoulder in time to absorb the impact instead of smacking into it face-first. The screech of metal wheels coming to an abrupt halt assaulted his ears as he whirled and snatched his Springfield from a corner. The door opened and a wide-eyed Linda Mather appeared.

"What happened, Clint?" she asked fearfully.

"They've stopped the train for some reason," he replied, working the carbine lever to chamber the first round.

"Don't leave me, Clint," she urged, clinging to his arm. "I'm frightened."

The Gunsmith wasn't certain what he should do under the circumstances, but the problem was soon solved when Roscoe, the porter, appeared at the mouth of the corridor. Clint asked him what was wrong.

"Lordy, what ain't, Mistah Adams?" the porter replied. "One of the engineers seen a feller fall offa the train so's he applied the brakes. Turns out it's one of them Mexican fellers. One of the two that was all dressed up fancy. He musta jumped offa the train and broke his neck when he fell 'cause he's deader than Mistah Abe Lincoln and John Wilkes Booth put together."

"Why would he jump off the train?" Clint inquired.

"Probably 'cause he figured Mistah Patterson woulda arrested him," Roscoe answered. "But ain't nobody been able to find Mistah Patterson. Nobody's even seen him for days. Has you seen him, suh?"

"No, I haven't," Clint admitted. "Why would the

Pinkerton arrest this *vaquero*?"

"Well, I don't imagine he would since the Mexican is dead . . ."

"All right," Clint sighed. "What did the man do that Patterson would have arrested him if he hadn't jumped off and broken his neck?"

"Why, he killed the other Mexican," Roscoe explained. "We found the other feller's body lyin' on a terrace between cattle cars. Guess them Mexicans had some sorta fight. Mighty mean folks them Mexicans. Look what them other fellers done yesterday. You was there, course . . ."

"How was the other *vaquero* killed" Clint asked.

"He was all cut up and stabbed a couple times," Roscoe answered. "Was the feller that was always playin' the guitar who got cut up. Couple of his fingers had been sliced off almost like the other feller, the one that jumped offa the train, had tortured him first."

"Tortured him?" Clint raised his eyebrows.

"Yessuh," the porter nodded. "Wouldn't expect that sorta thing from them fellers 'cause they seemed real nice and acted like they was good friends, but that Mistah Lloyd said Mexicans go sorta crazy when they's tryin' to prove how brave they are to each other."

"Lloyd told you that, huh?" the Gunsmith said dryly.

"Mistah Vargas said the same thing and he's part Mexican hisself, so I reckon he'd know."

"Yeah," Clint muttered. "I'm sure Vargas understands exactly what happened. Both he and Lloyd just happened to be awake and came out to explain all this to you after you found the bodies?"

"Yessuh, and Mistah Bruno was there too."

"The three of them are pretty close," Clint turned to Linda. "You might say they're thick as thieves. . . ."

She retreated into her room and closed the door.

". . . or killers," Clint whispered.

"What's that, suh?"

"Nothing, Roscoe," the Gunsmith assured him. Clint would have to have a talk with Stansfield Lloyd—soon.

NINETEEN

Bruno relieved Clint Adams of guard duty. The Gunsmith checked his quarters and found Vargas wasn't there. He left his Springfield. The .45 on his hip would be all he'd need for his "conversation" with Lloyd.

He found the pistolman in the dining car, eating breakfast and checking over a map with Vargas. Clint had expected to find the cross-breed with Lloyd. As long as he had his modified Colt, the knife artist wouldn't be much of a problem. The main threat was Stansfield Lloyd.

The gunman and Vargas looked up from their map when the Gunsmith entered the dining room. Clint glanced at the other patrons seated at surrounding tables. He didn't want them involved in what was about to happen, but he felt confident they'd leave when they saw a showdown in progress.

Clint approached the table with Lloyd and Vargas. "Why'd you kill them?" he asked bluntly.

Vargas's mouth fell open, but Lloyd's expression remained blank as he turned to Clint. "What are you talking about, Adams?"

"Ever since I joined this happy group, I've had a suspicion that there's more to this business than I've been told," Clint said. "I didn't like that very much, but when I have to kill men and I don't even know why, that gets me downright upset."

"You knew the job might call for killing," Lloyd replied. "Ain't nothin' new about that for you."

"Murder wasn't part of the deal," the Gunsmith stated.

"Murder? Them Mex sons of bitches—"

"Why'd you kill those two *vaqueros*?" Clint demanded. "Don't give me that fairy tale you told everybody else. Tell me the truth."

"And what do you figure the truth is, Adams?" Vargas asked, his hands disappearing under the table.

"Reach for a gun or a knife and I'll blow your head off," Clint warned him. "Keep your hands where I can see them. Both of you."

The passengers in the dining car had noticed that Clint stood before the table with his hand poised by the Colt on his hip. None of them could hear the conversation, but most guessed a confrontation had begun that might quickly lead to gunplay. Several left. Others watched with grim fascination.

"I don't think those *vaqueros* had a fight in a cattle car last night," Clint explained. "My guess is you two and Bruno paid them a visit in their sleeper, escorted them to the cattle car at gun point and tried to torture information out of them. Cutting off the guitar player's fingers sounds like your style, Vargas. Then you stabbed one of them to death and Bruno broke the other man's neck and threw him off the train."

"And what sort of information would we be askin' them about?" Lloyd inquired calmly.

"You probably figured they were associated with the eight men disguised as *peónes* who'd tried to break into Linda's room."

"Now, why would we figure that?" the gunman shrugged.

"I don't know," Clint admitted. "Just like nobody

seems to know what happened to Patterson either."

"Patterson?" Lloyd raised his eyebrows.

"The Pinkerton. He seems to have vanished."

"Can you prove any of this, Adams?" Lloyd asked with a grin.

"I've got enough evidence to clear my conscience if I have to shoot you both," Clint replied. "But all I want is the truth about this escort business."

Tension filled the dining car like an electrical mist. The Gunsmith and Lloyd locked eyes, each recognizing the cool professionalism of the other. Lloyd slowly slid back his chair and rose, his hand hovering close to the grips of his Remington revolver.

Without warning, glass shattered and a stocky passenger suddenly screamed when an arrow pierced his flabby belly. He clawed at the feathered shaft as he staggered backward and fell heavily on his rump. Feminine screams and masculine curses mingled with gasps.

"El Lobo!" Vargas exclaimed, scrambling from his chair.

Clint didn't worry when the cross-breed and Lloyd unsheathed their pistols. An Apache attack left no room for any personal confrontations if one wanted to survive. Clint's Colt was already in his hand as he moved quickly and cautiously toward the broken window.

Half a dozen brown-skinned riders mounted on bare-backed mustangs galloped along the side of the train. Clad only in loincloths, the Indians did not wear feathers or war paint and few carried firearms. *Apaches,* Clint thought. *Mescalero Apaches.* Mescaleros had gotten their name from their fondness for mescal. The band of warriors who'd attacked the train were excellent examples of why they had a reputation for being crazy even among other Apache tribes.

Led by the infamous Chintda, the band had seen the

great iron horse moving along the metal rails and regarded it as a gift from the gods. Mescalero in general
and Chintda's men in particular had always favored
plunder to hunting. Intoxicated on mescal, their drug-
fogged brains considered the bounty that awaited them
inside the train—white man's clothing, food, women
and weapons. They didn't concern themselves with the
fact that the last item might present an obstacle for trying to acquire the rest.

Chintda fancied himself a good strategist, so he told
his braves to wait until the iron horse began to climb a
hill, reasoning that the train would have to move slower;
this was the sum total of his tactics. The attack itself
lacked any organized effort or subtlety. Chintda and his
twenty-six followers charged the train on foot and
horseback, too crazy-brave to appreciate the folly of
their actions.

The Mescalero only had two things in their favor:
First, their assault was unexpected, and second the majority of the passengers weren't prepared to fight back.
Everyone on board had realized, however, that the train
would be traveling through Apache territory, and most
had brought at least one gun in case of such an attack.
Not all carried sidearms, but those who did opened fire
on the invaders while the others hurried to claim their rifles, carbines and shotguns.

Lloyd and Vargas shattered glass from windows with
the barrels of their revolvers and began shooting at the
Indians. Few carried anything more effective than a
single-shot muzzle-loader and most favored their tradi-
tional weapons. An arrow whistled past Lloyd's ear. He
ignored it as he calmly blasted an Apache off the back of
a mustang. Whatever else the pistolman might be, Clint
acknowledged, he wasn't a coward.

The Gunsmith didn't have any time to make further

evaluations of Lloyd or any of the other passengers' efforts to defend the train. A stone-headed tomahawk burst through a windowpane, followed by the dark arm and fierce face of its wielder. Clint's pistol roared and the Apache's features vanished in a spray of blood as the corpse hurtled away from the train.

Since there were several defenders within the dining car firing back at the Mescalero, Clint decided to head back to the passenger cars and see to Linda Mather's safety. As he left the dining compartment two Apaches came at him from the terraces between the cars.

One had an old Hawkens muzzle-loader while the other clutched a flint-bladed knife in one hand and a rather rusty .44 cap-and-ball Army Colt in the other as he awkwardly tried to climb over the railing without putting down either weapon. The Apaches' faces were lit up by the excitement of the raid. Clint noticed both of the mescal-happy morons grinned as if they'd just learned Santa had brought them everything they wanted for Christmas five months early—not that Mescalero believed in Santa Claus *or* Christmas. The brave who was trying to mount the platform actually giggled at his own clumsiness.

The Gunsmith didn't find the invaders amusing and even the intoxicated Apaches weren't about to laugh at the man with a gun in his hand. Before the Hawkens-toting brave could adjust the aim of his rifle, Clint squeezed the Colt's trigger. A .45 round tore through the Indian's chest and transformed his war whoop into a scream of agony before he toppled over the rail.

The other Apache snarled in rage and tried to launch himself at the Gunsmith, stabbing with his crude knife and swinging the revolver in his other fist like a tomahawk at Clint's skull. The Gunsmith nimbly dodged the knife thrust and blocked the pistol swing with his left

forearm. The muzzle of Clint's Colt jammed under the
Mescalero's chin and dug into the hollow of his jaw
when Clint squeezed the trigger again. The double-
action revolver blasted another bullet through the soft
flesh, piercing the roof of the Apache's mouth to tunnel
through his brain and blow off the top of his head.

Clint hopped to the next terrace, barely noticing the
Mescalero warriors that still galloped or ran alongside
the moving locomotive. A .50 caliber lead ball got his attention when it burst splinters from the side of the car
near his head. Clint bolted to the door and entered the
next compartment rapidly. An arrow slammed into the
door behind him.

He hadn't reached safety because danger didn't lurk
only *outside* the train. Four Mescalero had managed to
break into the passenger car. Three bloodied corpses—
two white and one Indian—already lay on the floor.
One Apache still stood over a victim with a smoking revolver in his fist. Another clubbed a kneeling figure with
a tomahawk.

The third had pinned the lovely young Mexican aristocrat to the floor. The still form of the matronly chaperon lay beside the struggling pair. The Apache ripped
at the girl's black lace dress as she tried to fight back.
Her efforts only amused the brute until she raked her
nails down a cheek, drawing blood and narrowly missing
an eye. Cursing in his guttural language, the Mescalero
responded by seizing the girl by the hair and slamming
the back of her head into the floor.

"Shit," Clint rasped as the closest Apache made eye
contact with him.

His face contorted with hatred, the Indian aimed the
pistol at the Gunsmith. Actually, he only lived long
enough to try before Clint's double-action Colt bellowed and a .45 slug sent the Apache hurtling backward
into a vacant seat.

The Gunsmith took two fast, long strides forward to reach the Mescalero who planned to rape the Mexican beauty. Even the Apache's lust hadn't occupied his attention enough to ignore the gunshot that had dispatched his companion to the Happy Hunting Ground. He raised his head with alarm and saw Clint advance.

The Mescalero reached for his war lance on the floor as he stared up at the white man. He wore his startled expression for less than a tenth of a second before Clint shot him in the face.

Clint hadn't forgotten the third Apache—or vice versa. He turned to discover the last brave had closed in quickly, his bloodied tomahawk raised high. The Gunsmith dodged the stone-bladed hatchet as he thrust the muzzle of his Colt into the Indian's stomach. The Mescalero's free hand slapped the pistol aside, more by accident than design, as Clint squeezed the trigger. A bullet grazed the Apache's hip, but the invader ignored the pain and swung his tomahawk again.

The Gunsmith raised his left hand in time to catch the wrist behind the crude hand-ax and simultaneously swung the now-empty Colt at the brave's head. Howling in fury and frustration, the Mescalero managed to block the attack and soon both men were locked in a deadly tug of war. Although the Mescalero was a head shorter than Clint and appeared to be underweight and malnourished, the man's scrawny frame was remarkably strong and tough in the manner of one bred to the hard life of an Apache.

Clint tried to drive a knee into his opponent's groin, striking a thigh muscle. The brave snarled and shoved harder, trying to pin the white man to the floor and use the tomahawk. Clint moved with the Apache, bending his knees as he fell to the floor.

The Mescalero's delight that he'd apparently gotten the upper hand in the struggle ended abruptly when he felt Clint's boot in his abdomen. Pulling the Apache's arms, the Gunsmith straightened his knee and watched the startled invader sail over his head.

The brave crashed to the floor in a stunned heap. Clint yanked his wrist free from the dazed Apache's grasp and allowed the .45 Colt to drop to the floor. His hands clawed at his shirt, the left yanking it open while the right reached inside.

The Apache rose to his feet first, eyes ablaze with rage and tomahawk poised for another attack. Suddenly, Clint's belly gun barked. A .22 hit the brave's chest. It startled the Mescalero more than it seemed to damage him since the Indian was too intoxicated and angry to feel pain.

Clint rolled on his side and fired twice more, putting two rounds into the Apache's forehead. Maybe the Mescalero still didn't feel the impact of the bullets, but he died anyway. Clint rolled out of the Indian's path as the brave fell to the floor.

"Josephia?" a feminine voice managed to creep through the Gunsmith's ringing ears.

The young Mexican beauty knelt beside her chaperon, one hand nudging the older woman as the other massaged the back of her own head. Clint slid his New Line Colt back inside his shirt and gathered up his .45 revolver before he got to his feet and approached the pair. He noticed the front of the girl's dress had been torn open and a cone-shaped breast protruded from the rip.

"Josephia?" she repeated, shaking the older woman, concern forming lines on her lovely features. The chaperon groaned weakly. *"Vives, Josephia. Gracias a Dios!"*

"Yeah," Clint agreed. His Spanish was pretty poor, but he understood most of her words. "Thank God we're all still alive." He opened the cylinders of his modified Colt and began ejecting spent cartridge casings. Clint gazed out the nearest window and saw a handful of Mescalero braves gallop into the distance. Only the dead remained.

"And thank you for coming to my rescue, señor," the girl said with a smile on her compact mouth.

He grinned in return as he fed fresh shells into the Colt. The woman's breast still peeked out of the girl's torn dress, its brown-capped nipple clearly visible.

"Are you and your friend all right, ma'am?" he inquired.

"Please, call me Sofia," she replied, slowly pulling her dress together. "And what is your name?"

"Adams!" a harsh voice supplied.

Clint turned to see Stansfield Lloyd standing at the door, his Remington .44 aimed at the Gunsmith.

TWENTY

"That game you played in the dining car wasn't very smart, Adams," the pistolman declared as he stepped closer. "Could be you caught a bullet during the injun raid, huh?"

"Could be," Clint nodded. The modified Colt in his hand was still open and contained three shells, all of them in position opposite of the movement of the weapon's double-action—in other words, Clint would have to close his pistol and squeeze the trigger three times before the first cartridge would be under the firing pin. Even he couldn't do this in less time than it would take Lloyd simply to pull the trigger once. "Of course, there's a witness who can say differently."

He cocked his head toward Sofia. The girl stiffened in fear when she saw the hard expression on Lloyd's face. Clint eased the cylinder of his Colt shut. Now, if he could jump to cover and either revolve the cylinder into position or pull the trigger three times, he and Lloyd would be on equal terms.

Then Lloyd canceled the need for such risky action by holstering his Remington. A cold smile slithered across his colorless lips. "We might still need you, Adams," he explained. "Reckon that earns you a re-preeve, don't it?"

"Gives one of us a reprieve anyway," Clint shrugged.

"You're good, Adams," Lloyd admitted. "But I reckon I can take you. We'll settle that after we reach Yuma. Meantime, you just keep your mouth shut. Understand?"

"I haven't needed a translator with you yet, Lloyd," the Gunsmith replied.

"Did you get a chance to check on Miss Mather?"

"Not yet."

Mike Vargas appeared at the threshold. He glared at Clint and fingered the ivory handle of his dagger. Lloyd glanced over his shoulder at his partner.

"Forget it, Mike," he ordered. "Adams is still one of us . . . more or less."

"Hopefully less," Clint muttered. "I'll go see to Linda now."

"We'll do it," Lloyd snapped. "You just keep away from her."

"Protecting her is my job," Clint stated. "Isn't it?"

"We'll talk about that later, Adams," the pistolman replied flatly.

Lloyd and Vargas marched through the passenger car. The latter cast a hateful stare at Clint. "When this is over," Vargas hissed, "you're dead, Adams."

Clint finished reloading his .45 Colt. Sofia observed him with unfettered interest.

"Your friends don't seem very happy with you, Señor Adams," she remarked.

"They aren't my friends," Clint answered. "We're just working together for a while," he grinned as he added. "And please call me Clint, all right?"

"Of course, Clint," she smiled.

"How's your friend?"

"The savage that tried to force himself on me hit her," Sofia explained. "But I don't think Josephia is truly injured."

The older woman now sat up, her back resting against a wall. She rubbed the side of her jaw and gazed up at Clint and Sofia with a trace of disapproval in her expression. The Gunsmith didn't blame Josephia for her opinion. She was Sofia's chaperon and responsible for the younger woman's safety and conduct. Fraternizing with a scruffy-looking gunman wasn't considered proper for a lady of breeding.

"You're escorting the woman who never leaves her room, no?" Sofia inquired. "She must be very important to merit such protection."

"I guess so," Clint shrugged. "If you ladies don't need me anymore, I'd better get back to work."

"Clint," she called to him as he headed for the door. "Beware of the company you keep."

"I have been," the Gunsmith rolled his eyes. "Believe me, I have been."

TWENTY-ONE

Seven passengers had been killed by the Mescalero raid and several others received injuries in the battle. Most of these were superficial cuts from the flying glass of broken windows, but two had been wounded by arrows and another caught a bullet in the forearm. Fifteen Indians had died in the carnage. The Apaches never reached Linda Mather's car.

The train stopped long enough to bury the slain passengers and unload the dead Mescaleros. No one suggested the raiders should receive a funeral, not even Reverend Kluger. The minister had startled his fellow passengers during the attack when he'd drawn a .44 Colt revolver from his valise and calmly opened fire on the Apaches.

" 'A time to love and a time to hate, a time of war and a time of peace'; Ecclesiastes, chapter two, verse eight," Kluger stated after the battle.

By three o'clock in the afternoon, the train was once again on its way to Yuma. None of the passengers would feel at ease until they reached their destination in the Arizona Territory. The terrain seemed to adopt a sinister appearance. Every rock formation and boulder threatened to conceal another band of hostile Indians. Even the occasional cottonwood tree and barrel cactus had acquired a new ominous quality.

Although Clint had never regarded the trip in a casual manner, he became even more cautious and apprehensive than before. The possibility of another Apache attack wasn't the primary source of his consternation. The likelihood of a second assault by loco Mescaleros was slim, but Lloyd and the others and the mystery about the true purpose for the escort team still ate at the Gunsmith like a bellyful of red ants.

The Gunsmith consulted his turnip-shaped watch, noting that it was time for Vargas to be on guard duty by Linda's door. That meant it should be relatively safe to return to his quarters and rest for a few hours. Clint hadn't slept much since the mission began and he knew he'd be getting even less sleep now. He headed for his compartment when a feminine voice softly called his name. He turned to see Sofia approach.

"I've been watching you walk back and forth through the train," she smiled. "You seem as restless as a caged lion."

"This isn't exactly a pleasure trip for me, ma'am," he replied dryly.

"My name is Sofia, remember?" the girl urged. "Perhaps I need to reinforce your memory so you won't forget me."

"I don't think that's apt to happen, Sofia."

"Let's make certain you remember," she said in a husky whisper. "I haven't properly rewarded you for your bravery yet, have I?"

"No need to," he answered a bit reluctantly, intrigued by the implication of her suggestion. "Unless you want to, of course."

"Come with me," Sofia declared simply.

He followed her into the sleeping cars. Sofia opened the door to her quarters and they entered. Clint closed the door, glancing about the room with appreciation. Like Linda Mather's quarters, it had obviously been furnished to appeal to a woman's taste, with a cedar chest of drawers, a full-length mirror and a four-poster bed. Two large steamer trunks more than five feet high stood on end serving as portable closets. Both were open a crack and Clint noticed the sleeves and hems of dresses that hung inside the luggage.

"A restless man should lie down once in a while," Sofia commented, tilting her head toward the bed.

"I've never been one to argue with a lady," Clint assured her, placing his Springfield in a corner.

Sofia stepped closer, lifting her face, eyes closed and lips parted in a silent challenge to just try to ignore her beauty. Clint didn't even try. He leaned forward and put his mouth against hers, his tongue sliding along the edges of her teeth. She chewed it gently, slipping her own tongue on the tip.

Their hands slowly explored each other. Clint caressed her firm breasts as the girl unbuttoned his shirt to slide eager fingers across his chest. They began to remove each other's clothing, still kissing and fondling as they undid buckles and buttons.

Naked, they moved to the bed. Sofia's stiff nipples jutted from her breasts in a sensuous invitation. The Gunsmith's mouth moved to them, kissing and sucking tenderly. The girl sighed with pleasure and lay back to allow him to mount her. Clint stroked her flesh slowly as Sofia's arms encircled his neck and pulled him closer.

"Love me, *mi héroe*," she whispered, wrapping her long legs around his thighs.

Although his maleness was already swollen and eager, Clint continued the foreplay, increasing the girl's excitement until she groped at his crotch to steer the hard organ into her wet cavern of love. The Gunsmith gradually moved himself back and forth, working his shaft deeper. The girl groaned and clung tightly to his body, begging for more. Clint obliged.

He failed to hear the creak of hinges when one of the steamer trunks opened behind them.

Clint increased the speed and force of his thrusts. Sofia arched her back to receive him, her limbs locked firmly around his hips and neck. The girl gasped in ecstasy when his organ exploded inside her.

Suddenly, Clint saw something out of the corner of his eye. He turned to see Josephia standing by the bed. The short, stocky chaperon's arms were rised high, both hands gripped the handle of a long-bladed dagger.

The Gunsmith tried to move to the side, but Sofia's arms and legs held him fast. The girl chuckled scornfully in his ear. "Die happy, *estúpido!*"

Josephia's arms plunged downward as Clint desperately hurled himself to the right. He rolled over on his back, taking Sofia's clinging body with him. The girl suddenly screamed. Her startled features, less than an inch from Clint's face, seemed to express more astonishment than pain.

The knife thrust intended for Clint Adams had claimed the wrong victim. Josephia hadn't been able to stop her attack in time and she'd driven the blade deeply between Sofia's shoulder blades. The older woman gasped in horror, yanking the dagger from the girl's trembling flesh.

Clint pried at Sofia's limbs, still locked around him even in death. The feel of her convulsing flesh made his nerves scream. Finally free of the dead woman's embrace, he pushed the corpse aside and leaped from the bed. Josephia had recovered from the shock of accidentally killing her fellow murderess. The woman shrieked with rage and attacked Clint.

The Gunsmith leaped away from the slashing blade. Josephia moved faster than her appearance suggested, her homely face twisted into a mask of animal fury as she thrust the dagger at Clint's dangling genitals. The tactic didn't surprise Clint. Women seem to have an instinct for going after a man's crotch—one way or the other. He caught her wrist in both hands and twisted hard, forcing her to drop the knife.

A dull click seemed to echo within the room. Clint saw the gleam of metal in Josephia's other fist. She'd drawn a Remington .41 caliber over-under derringer from somewhere in her gray gingham dress and thumbed back the hammer as a triumphant smile pulled her thick lips into a sneer.

Whoever said the female is the deadlier of the species, Clint thought, *knew exactly what he was talking about.*

Still holding Josephia's wrist in her right hand, Clint dropped to the floor. His left palm slapped the carpet as his legs shot out like a pair of giant scissors, trapping the woman's lower limbs. The Gunsmith rolled to the right, bringing the startled woman to the floor. Her cry of alarm was terminated by a muffled explosion when she hit the carpet—face first.

Josephia's body trembled violently. A small scarlet glob began to spread across her gray dress. She'd fallen on her own derringer and shot herself in the chest.

"Accident prone," Clint panted as he untangled himself from yet another lifeless woman's body.

The Gunsmith rose on unsteady legs. Knuckles rapped on the door and the conductor's voice demanded to know what had happened. Clint stumbled to the entrance and turned the knob, unconcerned about his nakedness as he yanked the door open. Andrew Waitley stared at Clint, his eyes bulging at the sight of a nude man in a lady's quarters.

"What—" the conductor stammered, "what are you—er—What was that shot?"

"End of a lesson, friend," Clint replied dryly. "I just learned that two women can be a bit too much for any man to handle."

TWENTY-TWO

Clint Adams had pulled on his clothes by the time Stansfield Lloyd and Mike Vargas appeared at Sofia's door. He wearily told the pair about the incident.

"Why would a *rica* do something like that?" Vargas asked dully, surprised by the tale.

"She weren't no rich bitch," Lloyd snapped, annoyed by his partner's naive remark. "She and the old toad was a pair of skirt-wearin' hootowls."

"Sofia lured me into her room to kill me because I'm part of Linda's escort," the Gunsmith said.

The pistolman glared at him. "What makes you say that, Adams?"

"Because it's pretty obvious she and Josephia killed Markham with the same tactic," Clint explained.

"Yeah," Lloyd agreed. "That explains why Jimmy was naked and stabbed in the back. He was havin' a good time with the young whore and the old one crept up behind him and used her knife."

"You still think those *peónes* that attacked us the other day were genuine?" the Gunsmith demanded.

"Reckon we'll never know if'n there was a connection between them and the two greaser gals since you killed both of the sluts."

"I didn't kill them exactly," Clint stated, trying to keep his temper. Killing women—no matter the reason—didn't sit right with him. "But I think you two already know the answer."

He turned to Vargas. "*El lobo* means *the wolf*, right?"

"Who said anything about El Lobo?" the cross-breed asked, his dark face contorted by anger.

"*You* did," Clint reminded him. "When the Mescalero attacked. Before you saw an arrow sticking in one of the passengers, you shouted *el lobo*. Now, why would you do a thing like that?"

"You got a longer nose than a shavetail jackass, Adams," Lloyd said in a hard voice. "And you're just about as dumb as one to be flappin' your gums all the time."

"A lot of people have been killed since we left Brownsville," Clint began. "I want to know why."

"You don't need to know nothin' except that you'll make three thousand dollars." Lloyd smiled coldly. "Ain't that enough?"

"It was when I took the job," Clint admitted. "But I've got a feeling I was hired under false pretenses and that doesn't sit well with me, Lloyd."

"That's too bad." The pistolman's smile froze into a dead man's grimace. "Reckon you can either quit and hand over the fifteen hundred dollars you was already paid or just stay pissed off until we reach Yuma."

"I've stuck it out so far." Clint shrugged. "But . . ."

Waitley, the conductor, led Roscoe and three male passengers into the sleeper to carry out the bodies of Sofia and Josephia. Clint had wrapped the younger woman in a sheet to conceal her nakedness. The grim-faced men hauled out their grisly burdens and the conductor cleared his throat as he summoned up enough courage to address the three gunmen.

"You gentlemen have been involved in entirely too

much violence since we left Brownsville," he began, trying to sound stern, but his eyes avoided the faces of the trio.

"Yeah," Lloyd snorted. "Like fightin' Apaches, huh?"

"That isn't the same as killing two female passengers," Waitley declared stiffly.

"Adams done that," Vargas smiled. "Talk to him about it."

The Gunsmith's eyes hardened. "I already told you what happened, Mr. Waitley. You seemed to believe me before. What changed your mind?"

"Well," the conductor hesitated. "I believe you, Mr. Adams, but some of the passengers are upset by what happened. . . ."

"The dagger and derringer that killed those two women belonged to them, not me," Clint said. "And I think the way Jimmy Markham was murdered a few days ago is ample proof to support my story. Could be, of course, you'd like to get us off this train and this is an opportunity to get the passengers to help you evict us."

Lloyd snorted. "Tell them greenhorns they're welcome to try to throw us off this train if'n they've got the sand for it. But you'd better warn 'em to send a whole lot of fellers 'cause a bunch of 'em are gonna be doin' some dying!"

"Let's all calm down a bit," Clint urged. "Mr. Waitley is just trying to keep his train from turning into a slaughterhouse. We can't blame him for that." Clint turned to the conductor. "We're almost in the Arizona Territory. Ask all those folks to be patient a little longer and they'll be rid of us when we reach Yuma. Until then, you might remind them that we're still traveling through Apache land. The Chiricahua aren't usually as crazy as the Mescalero, but they're a lot smarter and even more dangerous. You might still have reason to want us on this train before the trip is over."

"You have a good point, Mr. Adams," Waitley nodded quickly, eager to get away from the gunmen. "I'm certain everyone will be willing to wait until we get to Yuma . . . providing there's no more violence involving you and the other passengers."

"Violence is like a flash flood," the Gunsmith commented. "You can't guess when it's going to happen. All you can do is watch for the rain and hope things don't get out of hand, but you also try to be ready just in case it does."

"Ain't that pretty talk," Vargas sneered, shaking his head. "Makes me wanta puke."

"I know the feeling," Clint assured him.

"Like you say, Adams," Lloyd began. "We're almost at our destination, so I'm changing the rules a bit. I don't want you nowheres near Linda Mather. From now on, Mike, Bruno and me will handle sentry duty. You don't get involved with us again unless you hear shootin'."

"It sounds like my job just got easier," Clint shrugged. "Oh, Mr. Waitley?"

"Yes, sir?" the conductor asked, a pained expression on his face. He'd already spent more time with the trio than he cared for—in fact, he wished he'd never set eyes on any of them.

"Sophia and Josephia already paid for their room in advance, correct?"

"It was part of the price of their tickets," Waitley confirmed.

"Then nobody should object if I move into it," Clint smiled. "I'd just feel more comfortable if I had a room to myself. I think I'll sleep better that way."

"If that's what you want, Mr. Adams," Waitley agreed as he hurried away.

"I'd better move my gear," Clint told Lloyd and Vargas. "Looks like all of us have a private room now. Hope you two can stand the company you'll be keeping."

With that, he headed down the corridor. Vargas watched him depart and scowled. "When this is over, I'm gonna kill him!"

"Why wait that long?" Stansfield Lloyd asked.

TWENTY-THREE

Thick strands of black smoke from the locomotive engine chimney laced the night sky like whispy, dark rain clouds. Clint watched the stars and half moon try to peek through the sooty fog. The heavenly bodies had existed long before the invention of the train and they'd still be around long after the old diamond-stack iron horse became obsolete.

The Gunsmith opened his pocket watch. Almost midnight. He'd slept earlier, as well as his troubled mind would allow. His conscience had been giving him fits because he knew there was something wrong about the people he'd mixed in with at Brownsville. He didn't have enough information to put it all together, but he had decided where he could find some answers. His plan still contained a generous portion of risk, but Clint couldn't continue to be part of this business. If a man isn't able to live with himself and uphold his personal principles, then he might as well stuff a gun barrel in his mouth and pull the trigger.

He put out the flame to his lamp and moved through the dark room to the door. After a cautious glance to be certain the hallway was empty, he slipped out and closed the door.

The corridors and passenger cars of the train were all but deserted as he marched through them in a deceptively casual manner. His loose-limbed stride belied taut nerves and senses primed to full-alert. He scanned every empty seat and dark corner as though it might conceal a hidden adversary—because it was just possible one might.

However, the Gunsmith encountered no one more threatening than Roscoe. The porter was busy sweeping a passenger car with an old broom when Clint entered the compartment.

"Evenin', suh," Roscoe greeted with a smile.

"Hello, Roscoe," Clint replied softly. "Quiet night?"

"So far, suh," the porter nodded, but his tone expressed fear that that condition might soon change.

"Has anybody else been taking a stroll tonight?"

"None that's passed by me, Mistah Adams," Roscoe assured him.

"Do me a favor, Roscoe," Clint asked. "If anybody *does* pass by later, you haven't seen me, all right?"

"Why, I've been plum busy here cleanin' up the place," the porter shrugged. "What do I know 'bout anybody walkin' around after most folks is asleep."

"Thanks, Roscoe," Clint grinned.

"You take care, suh," the porter nodded in reply.

"I'll try."

Clint continued moving from car to car until he located the one that contained Linda Mather's compartment. He stood on the narrow platform outside, left hand poised on the door knob as the right unsheathed his .45 Colt. Taking a long, deep breath, he yanked the door open.

Mike Vargas stood guard duty in front of Linda's door. He stared in dumbfounded surprise at the Gunsmith. Clint's pistol pointed at Vargas's chest before the cross-breed could reach for a weapon. Clint cocked the revolver. The click of the double-action hammer filled the corridor.

"Step away from the Winchester," Clint instructed, making it clear that he'd noticed Vargas's rifle propped in a corner. "Raise your right hand and keep it over your head. Left hand only, unbuckle your gunbelt."

The cross-breed obeyed, slowly unfastening his belt and dropping it to the floor. His ivory-handled dagger was also in a sheath attached to the belt. The initial shock of the incident wore off and Vargas's features stiffened with anger, his eyes ablaze with hatred. However, he kept his right hand high and raised his left after completing Clint's instructions.

"You're doing fine," Clint remarked as he moved closer. "Keep it up and you might get to live to see the sunrise."

"What do you think you're gonna do?" Vargas asked stiffly, a thread of fear in his voice.

"We're going to have a talk with Miss Mather," Clint replied, easing the hammer down to uncock his Colt.

Of course, there was no need to touch the hammer of a double-action weapon. Clint had done so for purely psychological reasons. When he cocked the weapon, it emphasized to Vargas that the threat of death if he failed to obey was very real, and by uncocking it Clint seemed to imply that he wouldn't kill the man unless he had to. The Gunsmith wanted Vargas to relax a bit so he'd be off guard.

"It isn't polite to enter a lady's room without knocking first," Clint explained. "You do the honors, Vargas."

"Honors?"

"*Llama a la puerta, estúpido,*" Clint rasped.

Vargas turned to face the door and prepared to carry out the command. Clint hit him hard with the barrel of his Colt behind the right ear. The cross-breed groaned softly and crumbled to the floor.

Clint scooped up Vargas under the arms and dragged him to a corner. He wished he had some rope, but Vargas wouldn't regain consciousness for a while and Clint hoped he wouldn't need too much time.

However, he didn't intend to leave any weapons handy in case Vargas awoke ahead of schedule. He gathered up the cross-breed's Winchester rifle and gunbelt and then searched his unconscious opponent for hold-out weapons. He found a small knife concealed in a boot sheath and a spear-point blade with a leather-wrapped handle—a throwing knife—hidden in a pouch at the nape of Vargas's neck. Clint carried the guns and knives to the end of the car and hurled them into the darkness beyond the moving train.

The Gunsmith checked Vargas to be certain he didn't need another rap on the head to remain in dreamland for a while and then headed for Linda's door and knocked. It soon opened a crack.

"Good evening, ma'am," he greeted with an exaggerated formal nod.

"Clint!" Linda's beautiful face displayed surprise when she stared at the unexpected visitor. "I thought—that is—what do you—"

"Isn't your invitation still good, hon?" Clint asked as he firmly pushed the door forward.

She didn't try to stop him from entering. A smile appeared on her lush lips. "If you're feeling more loving, I'll be happy to have you stay for a while."

"Actually, I feel pretty upset about a lot of things," the Gunsmith said, closing the door. "I've been told a pack of lies from the start and I'd better get some truthful answers to some questions."

"Oh, Clint," Linda laughed gently. She turned slowly, allowing the lamplight to silhouette her shapely figure through the thin fabric of her pink nightgown. "Do we have to talk about this?"

"Why was I hired for this trip?" he demanded. "What do Lloyd and the others—including *you*—know that I don't? What are we really protecting?"

"You're suppose to be protecting me," Linda stepped closer. "Don't you think I'm worth it?"

"We've been protecting *something* in this room, but it isn't you," Clint declared flatly. "The day the false *peónes* attacked, I'd met you and Lloyd in the dining car having lunch. Remember that?"

"And you escorted me back to my room and we made love. . . ." She started to snake her arms around his neck.

Clint slipped away from her embrace. "Bruno was still stationed at the door, Linda. Why was he guarding this room when you weren't in it?"

"Ask Stan," the girl replied. "He's in charge of that stuff."

"I'm asking you."

"I don't have an answer," she started to slip the straps of her gown from her shoulders. "Why are we wasting time talking like this?"

"Who is El Lobo?" the Gunsmith asked.

Linda raised her face toward his, eyes closed and lips parted to invite a kiss. Clint wanted to respond to her, but realized that was exactly what she wanted. Linda used her charm and her beauty as a weapon. When his lips failed to meet hers, Linda opened her eyes to see Clint shaking his head.

"You'd better answer me," he told her.

"What if I don't?" Linda challenged. "What are you going to do? Slap me around for a while?"

"I'll leave that for Stan Lloyd to take care of," Clint said dryly.

She raised an eyebrow. "You do pay attention, don't you?"

"I try," Clint tilted his head toward her steamer trunks. "Why is one of those all padlocked like a treasure chest, Linda?"

Her eyes opened wide in surprise.

"Open it," he instructed.

Then a hard metal cylinder jabbed into the small of his back. "You're getting a might too pushy, Adams," Stansfield Lloyd's voice rasped near his ear.

"Guess the company I've been keeping lately has made me a little antisocial," Clint replied, raising his hands over head.

TWENTY-FOUR

With the pistolman's Remington stuck in his spine, there wasn't much Clint could do except go along with Lloyd's game—for now.

"We'll have to learn you some manners, won't we?" Bruno's gruff voice added. The big bald man stepped from behind Clint. He held his S&W .44 revolver in one huge hand as the other plucked the modified Colt from Clint's holster.

"You all right, Linda?" Lloyd inquired. He pressed the muzzle of his pistol harder against Clint's back. "Did this bastard hurt you?"

"Hardly." Linda smiled sadly. "That's not his style."

"Lucky we decided to check on Mike," Lloyd remarked. "When we found him lyin' in a corner on the floor, we figured Adams was up to something."

"What an astute deduction," Clint muttered dryly.

"Just couldn't leave it be, could you, Adams?" Bruno commented, thrusting Clint's Colt into his belt.

"Let's get rid of him," Lloyd said. "Quietly."

"Well, don't kill him in my room, for crissake!" Linda snapped.

"Course not," the pistolman assured her. "Adams is gonna get off the train ahead of schedule."

"Yeah," Bruno smiled. "With a busted neck!"

"Move!" Lloyd's Remington shoved forcibly into the Gunsmith's spine.

Clint turned toward the open door, his arms still held high as he walked to the exit with his captors. *You really don't have a thing to lose,* he told himself.

Suddenly, he whirled. His left arm swung low, sweeping Lloyd's gunhand toward the floor while his right fist lashed into the pistolman's face. He quickly shoved Lloyd into Bruno, trying to keep both men off balance. Neither fired a weapon. *They don't want any shooting,* Clint thought, finding some comfort in the realization.

The Gunsmith grabbed Lloyd's arm and shoved it down to meet his knee which rose to strike the man's wrist hard. Lloyd's Remington popped from his grasp and fell to the floor. Clint slashed the back of his fist into the stunned gunman's face, knocking Lloyd backward four feet.

Bruno's enormous shape rushed forward, his S&W held by the barrel as he swung the walnut grips like a hammer at Clint's head. Clint met the big man's charge, hands flashing out to seize the attacking arm.

The Gunsmith pivoted, using Bruno's own momentum to pull him forward and placed the arm on his shoulder. He bent swiftly and sent the startled brute hurtling over his back in an unexpected Flying Mare. Bruno's body slapped the floor hard. Still holding the arm captive, Clint raised a boot and stomped it into the big man's armpit. Bruno screamed as the nerve cluster under his arm seemed to burst. His S&W fell from numb fingers before Clint could grab it.

Lloyd's arms suddenly encircled Clint's upper torso and arms, trying to apply a bear hug from behind. Clint rammed an elbow into the pistolman's solar plexus. Lloyd groaned and released Clint. The Gunsmith's elbow rose and crashed into the point of Lloyd's jaw. The pistolman fell to the floor.

Suddenly, Bruno's fist filled Clint's vision a moment

before it connected with his face. The punch sent him staggering backward to topple unceremoniously over the top of the small table in Linda's room. He fell against one of the chairs and took it with him to the floor.

His head filled with shards of agony, eyes covered by crimson cataracts, Clint stared up to see a nine-foot tall bald-headed monster marching toward him. The Gunsmith knew he couldn't trade punches with Bruno. He had to take out the big man somehow—fast.

Clint rose to his feet, the chair in his grasp. He raised the furniture for a shield as Bruno threw another punch. The chair quivered in Clint's hands and wood cracked. Bruno's fist had shattered the chair seat. Clint quickly kicked Bruno in the abdomen. The big man grunted and bent slightly. The Gunsmith ripped the chair from Bruno's arm and swung it with all his might, breaking what remained of the furniture across the brute's broad back.

Bruno was knocked across the room by the blow. Clint reached for his shirt, trying to get his New Line Colt out of his belt, but Lloyd had once again returned to the melee. He clasped his hands together and chopped them into the Gunsmith's back between the shoulder blades. The unexpected blow knocked Clint to the floor. He landed on all fours, his right hand close to a broken chair leg.

Lloyd drew back a boot, prepared to launch a kick at Clint's head. The Gunsmith slashed the chair leg into the pistolman's shin before the foot could connect. Lloyd hopped backward and howled with pain as Clint scrambled to his feet. The Gunsmith quickly rammed one end of his improvised club into the gunman's belly and followed up with a left hook to the side of his head. Lloyd fell to the floor once more and didn't get up.

Clint turned in time to see Bruno charge forward, massive hands arched like the talons of a killer eagle. Desperately, Clint sidestepped the murderous lunge and thrust the chair leg between the brute's attacking arms. He felt the end of the club stab into something soft. Suddenly, Bruno staggered away from him, both hands clutching his throat. The big man's eyes swelled in alarm and pain as blood bubbled up from his crushed trachea to spill from his lips. Then he crumbled to the floor and died.

Stunned by his stroke of luck against the giant, Clint turned slowly to check on Lloyd. The pistolman groaned feebly, but he wasn't ready to get frisky yet. Then Clint remember Linda Mather . . . too late.

He sensed someone's presence behind him and heard the rush of air being cut by a heavy, rapidly moving object. Clint's skull seemed to explode into a white burst of agony. He didn't feel the impact when his unconscious body fell to the floor. . . .

TWENTY-FIVE

Clint Adams knew he was still alive. He didn't have firsthand knowledge, but he was pretty sure the dead didn't feel pain.

Every inch of his body ached. The Gunsmith's jaw was painfully swollen and his skull felt as if it was filled with hot coals. Clint's torso and limbs were sore and his face seemed to be on fire. As memories slowly returned with consciousness, he wondered where he was. Clint realized he was lying on his back in something soft. Surely he couldn't be on the train.

Clint tried to open his eyes. The lids seemed to be covered with lead. When they finally parted, a bolt of flame pierced his eyes and Clint groaned hoarsely in response.

Suddenly, a black shape blotted out most of the glare and a voice declared, "*Luis! Éste no es muerto!*"

More figures moved around the Gunsmith as his vision began to clear. They were men, dressed in tattered cotton clothing with bandoliers full of ammunition crisscrossing their chests and straw sombreros on their heads. One of them, a thickly built Mexican with an unkempt beard and a cigar butt in his yellow teeth, bent over to examine Clint more closely.

"How about it, *gringo*?" he asked with amusement, his English heavily accented. "Is Raul right for a change? You alive, *gringo*?"

"Sort of," Clint croaked weakly.

"*Sí*," the man puffed his cigar and smiled. "Maybe not for long. We found that bald *bastardo* Bruno lying over there," he jerked a dirty thumb to his left. "But he's dead. You know that?"

"Yeah," Clint rasped, his throat felt as if it was filled with sand. "I killed him."

"Oh?" the Mexican sounded impressed. "How did you do this, Señor Gringo?"

"I jabbed a chair leg into his throat," Clint replied.

"*Muy bien!*" the man declared with delight. "I wondered what had happened to him. You must be a tough *hombre,* no?"

Clint slowly sat up, his body a mass of aches and needlelike pains. "I sure don't feel very tough, Señor—?"

"I am Luis Mendez," the Mexican stated, his black eyes narrowed. "Maybe you heard me called El Lobo."

"The Wolf," Clint nodded weakly. He glanced at his own shirt front and trousers in the process. His clothes were splattered with mud.

"So your back wasn't broken when they threw you off the train, *gringo*," Mendez observed. "You and Lloyd have a falling out, eh?"

"We never really had a falling in to begin with," Clint reached to the back of his head to rub his throbbing skull and discovered his hair was matted with mud. "Where am I?"

"You're in the middle of nowhere." El Lobo shrugged. "Oh, you *gringos* call it Arizona and I guess the Apache call it something else, but I think nowhere is good enough for where we are."

Clint strained stiff muscles to rise to his feet. He found himself standing in a pool of mud. Apparently, Lloyd and Vargas had thrown him off the train and by an incredible stroke of good fortune, he'd landed in the wet ooze. It was probably the only mud hole for miles in the heart of the desert and it saved Clint from a fall that might otherwise have broken his back in two.

"Getting up already," Mendez nodded. "Tough *hombre*."

Clint glanced about. There were nine other men with El Lobo, each as dirty and vicious in appearance as Mendez. All were heavily armed with one or more revolvers, big fighting knives and rifles or shotguns. *Bandidos*, Clint thought, *and probably even meaner than they look*.

Mendez suddenly reached for an ivory-handled pistol on his right hip. Clint's hand automatically flashed to his right hip, but his gunbelt and modified Colt revolver were gone. El Lobo dragged his gun from leather, aimed it at Clint and thumbed back the hammer.

"Even a tough *hombre* like you can be killed, *gringo*," Mendez sneered. "You know any reason I shouldn't shoot you?"

"Why do the Anglo a favor, Luis?" another *bandido* remarked, drawing a thick bladed Bowie knife from a belt sheath. "Let's make the pig squeal."

"*Sí*, Raul," Mendez smiled. "Maybe you're right about something else today."

"Hold on a minute," Clint began. "If you want me to answer some questions there's no need to cut me up while you ask them."

"That so?" El Lobo uncocked his pistol and slid it back into its holster. "Maybe, 'cause I don't think you and Stan Lloyd are friends no more. But you was one of his gang, no?"

"No," Clint shook his head. "This is going to take a while to explain. May I have some water?"

"Polite as well as tough, eh?" Mendez remarked.

Then he ordered one of his men to give Clint a canteen.

The water was alkaline and bitter, but it tasted better than champagne to the Gunsmith. Careful not to gulp, he drank slowly and the water soothed his parched throat. He held the canteen as he explained how he'd been hired by Jacob Mather to escort the rancher's daughter from Brownsville to Yuma, occasionally taking more sips of water between sentences.

Before Clint could continue his story, Mendez and several of his men who understood English burst into laughter. El Lobo shook his head and smiled.

"Señor Gringo," he began, "you are either a very good liar or you've been a very great fool."

Clint didn't care for either title, but he wasn't in a position to complain about insults. "What do you mean, Mendez?"

"This Mather, he is a big man with gray hair. Acts like he thinks he's a general, no?" El Lobo inquired.

"You could describe him that way," Clint agreed, recalling the rancher's authoritative manner.

"His name isn't Mather," Mendez said. "He is Jacob Manning, formerly Colonel Manning in the Confederate Army. That *puta* Linda is not his daughter. She's Manning's mistress. *Comprende?*"

"I'm beginning to," Clint replied, taking another long swallow of water before returning the canteen to its owner. "But it sounds like we should compare notes, Señor Mendez."

"Me and my men don't exactly specialize in taking notes," El Lobo stated. "We're better at taking lives."

"I'll bear that in mind," Clint assured him.

TWENTY-SIX

Fortunately, the bandits had some extra mounts—ten horses, in fact. This number seemed significant to Clint, who recalled the eight false *peónes* and two female assassins he'd encountered on the train. After taking a Henry carbine from the saddle boot, the bandits allowed the Gunsmith to mount one of the spare horses.

El Lobo clearly didn't want Clint armed, which meant none of the *bandidos* had frisked him while he was unconscious because the New Line Colt was still tucked in his belt and hidden under his shirt. The little .22 belly gun wouldn't be much good against ten heavily armed men, but Mendez and his crew didn't intend to kill him . . . yet. The diminutive Colt was the only ace the Gunsmith had up his sleeve . . . or under his shirt.

Actually, he had one other item of value, one which under the circumstances was more vital than any weapon for his continued survivial. He had firsthand knowledge about Linda, Lloyd and the others on the train and the events that had occurred since they'd left Brownsville. This was probably the only reason Mendez had kept him alive. However, this knowledge could well be a two-edged sword, and if he wasn't careful, Clint could talk himself into an impromptu execution.

The Gunsmith and his *bandido* companions rode along the railroad tracks to the west. They were sur-

118

rounded by miles of sand, rocks and cactus, yet the terrain wasn't as formidable as it first appeared to Clint. He saw a number of "desert islands," raised mounds which usually meant there was water underground. Patches of vegetation and occasional cottonwood trees also reassured him that the environment wasn't quite as hostile to life after all.

"Why so many extra horses?" Clint asked Mendez as he rode beside the bandit leader.

"You ain't figured that out yet, Señor Gringo?" El Lobo asked.

"They belong to the eight men who were disguised as *peónes* who got on the train at El Paso?" Clint pretended to guess what he'd already deduced.

"Maybe you're not so stupid after all. What happened to them? Since they didn't meet me in Las Palomas, I figure something went wrong."

"They're dead," Clint replied simply. "Lloyd and the others killed them when they tried to storm Linda's quarters."

"You kill any of them, *gringo*?" Mendez glared at him.

"I didn't have any choice," Clint answered. "They were trying to kill me. What would you have done?"

"The same," Mendez admitted. His expression became troubled as he continued. "Two women also got on at El Paso. . . ."

Clint had expected this and prepared a reply. "A band of Mescalero Apaches attacked the train in New Mexico."

"I know," Mendez nodded. "We've been trailing the train since Las Palomas. We came across the dead *indios*. The savages killed Sofia and Josephia?"

"I'm sorry," Clint told him.

"Sofia was my woman," Mendez said sadly. "I have

two other women and neither of them are as treacherous as my Sofia was. She was a good woman for a *puta*. I will miss her.

"Guillermo will be brokenhearted to hear his wife is dead," Mendez added. "He is Josephia's husband. She was fat, ugly and vicious, but he loved her. Maybe he liked it when she beat him with a broomstick or a razor strap when she lost her temper at Guillermo."

"Maybe your men will have pity on him and treat him to a nice flogging at the funeral," Clint muttered under his breath.

"*Qué?*" Mendez asked.

"Just cursing out Lloyd for throwing me off that train and cursing myself for agreeing to the job in the first place," the Gunsmith answered.

He mentally cursed Lloyd and the rest for something he didn't bother to mention to Mendez. The two *vaqueros* they'd killed on the train hadn't been sent by the *bandidos*. The gunmen had murdered them just in case they were El Lobo's men.

"What's this about Mather really being an ex-Confederate colonel and Linda being his mistress?" Clint asked.

"*Coronel* Manning returned to his home in Georgia to find the Union soldiers—who were called Yankees, I am told. I had always thought all you *gringos* were Yankees." Mendez shrugged. "Anyway, the soldiers had taken over everything and Manning turned into an outlaw, but a clever one. He didn't rob banks and stagecoaches. Not Manning. He made certain the profit would be worth the risk and he always tried to hire the best men possible for any job he planned."

"Men like Stansfield Lloyd."

"*Sí,*" Mendez confirmed. "That one is famous for his fast gun. You met Vargas, the mongrel knife artist, no?

He is also a very deadly *hombre,* and although he hates his *mejicano* blood, he still knows my country and speaks the language like a native."

"Vargas seems to hate everybody and everything," Clint remarked. "Especially himself. How do you know so much about them?"

"Because they worked with me six months ago in Mexico," El Lobo answered bitterly. "Vargas knew about me, and Manning used him to contact us to see if we'd be interested in one of his schemes. By pretending to be a wealthy *gringo* businessman interested in buying coffee from the plantations in southern Mexico, Manning was able to rub shoulders with some influential *ricos* in Monterrey. One of these was a *federale* general who talked too much when he got drunk and wound up in bed with the *puta* Linda. He told her about a shipment of gold being transported from Monterrey to the national treasury in Mexico City."

Clint wished El Lobo would tell a story in the order that events happen, but he was able to follow Mendez's narrative.

"But the gold was being escorted by soldiers and Manning's group was too small to take it on alone," El Lobo continued. "That's why he contacted me and my men. Since there was a fortune in gold—worth almost a million *gringo* dollars—we accepted. The agreement was that Manning would split the profit with us fifty-fifty, no? But instead, he helped us set up the ambush and then he and his cutthroats stole the gold and left us to fight the soldiers who had scattered all over the rocks for cover after the shooting started. I once had fifty-six compañeros under my command. More than half of them were killed that day."

"And Manning fled across the border to the United States with the gold," Clint guessed.

"*Sí*," Mendez hissed. "I don't know how he found out I was trying to track him down, but he must have either known or suspected, because when we arrived in Texas, he had already gone."

"And the gold was on board a train bound for Yuma with Linda 'Mather' and her escort team."

"And Manning left Brownsville too," Mendez declared. "Probably on horseback, figuring we wouldn't try to find him since we're more interested in the gold. As if we need to look for him." The bandit grinned. "He'll be waiting for them in Yuma. The train has to stop too often to get fuel, pick up freight and passengers. A man on horseback can move faster if he doesn't mind pushing a mount. You'll see. In a couple days we'll catch up with the train ourselves because horses can go across prairies and hills that don't have iron rails laid down."

"You know a short cut, eh?" the Gunsmith inquired.

"That's right," Mendez nodded. "I'd sent a telegram to my men in Monterrey and told them to get on board the train at El Paso and get the gold, but that didn't work. So, now, I'll take care of that *cabrón* Manning personally and reclaim the gold that is rightfully mine. Don't you agree?"

"Sure," Clint lied. "You stole it. Who else would it belong to?"

"And my *compañeros* died fighting to get it," Mendez said fiercely. Then he glared at Clint with suspicion. "How come they threw you off the train?"

Clint formulated a story that contained mostly truth. "It didn't take long for me to realize they had something that was worth a lot more than her body. I'd just about had things figured out when the others turned on me."

"How many men does Lloyd have on the train with him?"

"Five of us left Brownsville with Linda," Clint answered. "Bruno and Markham are dead and I was . . .fired last night so that leaves Lloyd and Vargas—plus Manning and whoever he might have with him."

"That don't sound like too much of a problem," El Lobo mused, scratching a match to life on the horn of his saddle. He lit the cigar between his teeth. "I've lost a lot of men, not to mention poor Sofia and Josephia. I've got a lot of things to make Manning pay for. How about you?"

"I want Lloyd," Clint said flatly.

"He's very good with a gun, Señor Gringo. . . ."

"Just let me have Lloyd and get my belongings that are still on that train," Clint insisted. "You can have the rest."

El Lobo smiled slyly. "And you don't want a share of a million dollars in gold?"

"Who wouldn't?" Clint grinned in reply. "But I figure that'll depend on whether or not you're feeling generous after we've settled scores with those bastards."

"I'm being pretty generous just letting you live, *gringo*," Mendez commented. "And that's a condition that can be changed just like that." El Lobo snapped his fingers to serve as an example.

"I know," Clint assured him. *What fun traveling companions I've been getting lately,* he thought.

TWENTY-SEVEN

To Clint's surprise, El Lobo and his men headed across the prairie toward a small collection of adobe huts with half a dozen horses contained in a rope corral.

"We'll spend the night here," Mendez declared. "It used to belong to a bunch of Pueblo *indios,* but we sort of convinced them to let us use it."

"Yeah," the Gunsmith replied, trying to conceal his loathing for the bandits' tactics. "But why waste time here? What if the train makes better time than you've counted on and arrives in Yuma ahead of schedule?"

"Because we don't like to ride horses in the dark," El Lobo told him. "They can step in prairie dog holes and break their legs—and a rider can break his neck falling off a horse too. Besides, this is still Apache territory. Those *hijos del Diablo* are bad enough in the daylight; I don't want to go up against them at night."

"You're making the decisions, *jefe,*" Clint shrugged, addressing the bandit boss as "chief."

Mendez smiled, pleased with the remark. "Don't worry, Señor Gringo. Even if the train gets to Yuma before we do, we won't have much trouble finding Manning and his followers. They won't be able to go very far with all that gold and they're a pretty strange-looking group so people will remember them. Those *cucarachas* won't get away from me again."

Clint didn't bother to remind El Lobo that he was more concerned about his property on the train than the gold or revenge. Virtually everything he owned was on that train—his wagon, his clothes, his tools. What worried him most was the possibility of losing Duke. The big black gelding was more than a horse to Clint. Duke was a partner and a friend.

He also wanted his modified Colt .45 back. The double-action revolver was a one-of-a-kind gun. It had taken Clint years of trial and error to finally perfect his pistol. To try to make another one would be a monumental feat. Besides, he didn't like the idea of a lowlife like Lloyd or Vargas taking possession of his prize creation.

There was no point in trying to explain any of this to El Lobo. The bandit leader was so hardhearted he barely seemed to care about the death of Sofia who had been one of his women. As long as Clint rode with the bandits, he'd have to go along with Mendez's rules and watch for an opportunity to break away from the gang.

A thin gray-haired man with dark Latin features— that may have been handsome if his face hadn't been frozen into an expression of dour hopelessness— stepped from one of the adobe huts. Three younger, less solemn men also rushed forward to meet El Lobo and his band. When the riders reached the camp and dismounted, the trio helped them lead the horses to the corral. The gray-headed man still stood by the adobe dwellings, his eyes wide and his expression even more sorrowful than before.

"That's Guillermo," Mendez informed Clint. "He's noticed we didn't return with his precious Josephia," El Lobo clucked his tongue with disgust.

A tall, hawk-faced man with fierce dark eyes brushed past Guillermo as he marched toward Mendez and

Clint. The man looked mean enough to chew iron ore and spit out roofing nails. He sure carried enough firepower—a holstered revolver on each hip and a third thrust into his belt.

"*Quién es, el gringo?*" he demanded angrily.

"Our guest is an *hombre* who has no love for Manning and his gang," Mendez answered. "And he doesn't speak *español* very well so talk English, Tomas." El Lobo turned to Clint. "Tomas is my *teniente*— lieutenant."

"What happened to our men, Luis?" Tomas asked, glaring at Clint with unconcealed hostility. "And why you bring this Anglo back?"

"I'll explain everything to you later," Mendez replied. "For now, I'm going to tell Maria and Rosanna that they will no longer have Sofia to fight with. You put Señor Gringo in the *cárcel* and don't hurt him unless he gives you trouble."

"*Sí,*" Tomas replied, drawing a pistol. From his expression, Clint guessed Tomas would like to have an excuse to use his gun. "Come with me, *gringo.*"

"Luis?" Guillermo began, slowly approaching the bandit chief as Mendez stomped toward one of the adobe huts. "*Donde está Josephia?*"

"*Muerta,*" Mendez replied, not even breaking stride as he told Guillermo his wife was dead.

Clint heard the gray-haired man wail in grief and saw him bury his face in his hands and weep as he slowly sank to his knees in the dirt.

"I'm glad Luis broke the news to him gently," the Gunsmith muttered sourly.

"Hey, *gringo,*" Tomas barked. "I tell you to come with me, no? You refuse and I shoot you. *Comprende?*"

"Don't get excited," Clint urged. "I'm ready to go with you. Okay?"

Tomas escorted Clint through the tiny adobe hamlet. The Gunsmith noticed the *bandidos* had wasted little time locating tacos, tortillas and tequila. He saw a group of them ravaging the food and liquor and realized his own stomach growled for attention.

"Will I get any food, Tomas?" he inquired.

"You'll get a bullet if you don't move!" the bandit lieutenant snapped. "And you will address me as *teniente, gringo!*"

Clint almost asked him why he wanted to be called *teniente gringo* but decided Tomas didn't have much of a sense of humor. Then a movement at one of the adobe structures caught his eye and he glanced into the face of a lovely young girl who stood in the doorway of the hut.

She was clearly very young, under sixteen. Small and yet to develop a full bosom, her face was the greatest attraction, with its large doelike brown eyes and wide, full mouth. The girl's jet-black hair framed her oval face and she offered Clint a wide grin and a suggestive wink before Tomas shoved him toward a small adobe structure, about the size of an outhouse.

"This is the *cárcel, gringo,*" Tomas declared.

"Charming," Clint muttered. "What is a *cárcel*, anyway?"

"It means jail, *estúpido!*" the bandit growled as he pushed Clint through the canvas curtain that served as a door to the tiny building.

The *cárcel* was simplicity itself: four hard adobe walls with a ceiling, a dirt floor and the "door" he'd been shoved through. No furniture or windows. He wondered what the Pueblo Indians had used it for and guessed it had once stored grain for the tribe.

But whatever it had been, for Clint it was jail and there didn't seem to be much he could do about it. He guessed what he'd see when he pulled back the curtain and peeked outside, but he checked anyway.

A hard-faced *bandido* was stationed at the entrance. The man gestured at Clint with the barrel of an old Spencer carbine, warning him to stay where he was. Clint nodded in response, closed the curtain and sat down in the dark, cramped cell.

"Stone walls do not a prison make," he mused. "Adobe with an armed guard will work just as well."

TWENTY-EIGHT

"You comfortable, Señor Gringo?" Luis Mendez inquired as he pushed back the curtain and poked his head into the *cárcel*.

Clint resisted an urge to put his fist in El Lobo's grinning face. "Why the hell did you put me in here?"

"Two reasons," Mendez began. "First, I don't want you sneaking around my camp and maybe causing trouble. I don't trust nobody. I've stayed alive that way. If I was going to trust somebody, it wouldn't be an Anglo like you. The other reason is I don't want one of my men to get drunk and decide to shove a knife between your ribs. I don't want you killed. . . . At least, not yet."

"Your hospitality overwhelms me," Clint said dryly.

"If you need to shit, let the guard know," Mendez chuckled. "Now, my women are waiting for me to satisfy their desires. Any questions before I go?"

"I suppose it would be asking too much to be able to get enough water to wash up a little." His hair and clothes were still caked with mud. "And maybe a clean shirt if you can spare it."

"You're right, *gringo*," Mendez smiled. "That's too much to ask. We're in the middle of a desert, remember? We can't waste no water on bathing.

"I noticed," Clint muttered. "How about something to eat then?"

"Maybe." Mendez shrugged. "If there's enough left after my men are through. Anything else?"

Clint shook his head.

"Have a nice night, Señor Gringo," Mendez laughed as he withdrew from the door of the *cárcel*.

El Lobo had never bothered to ask Clint what his name was, content to address him as Señor Gringo. Mendez and the others regarded him as a bottom-of-the-barrel gunhand who'd been duped by Manning. Clint didn't want them to change their opinion because so far none of them had bothered to search him. He still had his New Line Colt and fifteen hundred dollars in a money belt.

The Gunsmith tried to ignore the growling in his stomach and decided to take advantage of the privacy of his cell to check his belly gun and pocket watch. As he'd feared, the latter had suffered from the fall of the train. The crystal was cracked and the minute hand had broken off. He hoped the pistol would be in better shape.

Removing the New Line from its hiding place under his shirt, Clint inspected the frame and cylinders, pleased to discover the gun hadn't been dented or clogged with mud. He held the little gun close to his ear and eased back the hammer. It clicked into place smoothly and he didn't hear the grating sound of sand or dust within the parts. Clint uncocked the Colt, found the trigger operated fine, and then checked the barrel to be sure it wasn't bent and the muzzle wasn't plugged up.

Satisfied that the little .22 would be ready if he needed it, Clint put the belly gun away and tried to make himself as comfortable as possible on the dirt floor. If he couldn't eat or bathe, perhaps he could at least get some sleep.

He fell into his "combat-ready" slumber, his hands folded on his stomach close to the hold-out gun under his shirt. For three hours, he rested in this manner until the rustle of the curtain tugged at his consciousness.

"Señor," a voice whispered gently.

Clint awoke immediately, his nostrils twitching from the scent of chili and tacos. He sat up and saw a small, slightly built figure at the entrance of the *cárcel*. There was just enough light available in the dim cell to allow him to recognize the big dark eyes and wide smile of the girl he'd seen before Tomas shoved him into the jail.

"I brought you food, señor," she whispered.

"I can smell it," Clint replied. "It's as welcome as your smile, señorita. *Muchas gracias.*"

The girl entered the cell and knelt next to him. The quarters were compact and there was little enough room for Clint let alone the girl. Her chest pressed against his left triceps as she handed him a plate of tacos and a clay bowl of *chili con cabra-carne*. He tried to move away from her small breasts that pressed against his arm, but there wasn't enough room in the cell and the girl didn't attempt to shift away from him.

"My name is Carla," she declared with a broad grin that accented her cushiony full lips.

"I'm Clint," the Gunsmith responded to the introduction. "You speak very good English, Carla. Where'd you learn it?"

"From my father and Uncle Luis," she answered.

"El Lobo is your uncle?" Clint was startled to learn that the bandit chief would risk his niece's life by exposing her to the dangers involved in his line of work. Carla's virginity was in even greater jeopardy since she was a very pretty girl surrounded by unprincipled and immoral men.

"*Si*,"Carla confirmed. "And Guillermo is my father."

"Luis's brother?" Clint recalled El Lobo's callous attitude when he told Guillermo about the death of his wife Josephia. "Oh, I'm sorry about your mother, Carla."

"No need," the girl assured him, pressing her body closer to his. "She was—how do you say in English? A bitch?"

"Carla . . ." Clint didn't know how to respond to her remark. "You shouldn't talk that way about your mother."

"Why?" The girl's fingers coasted across Clint's chest. "She used to beat me. Mama hated me because I am not fat and ugly like she was. She beat my father too. He cries for her. Let him shed tears for us both."

Clint moved the bowl of chili to his abdomen to block the path of Carla's hand before it brushed against his belly gun. "Won't your father and uncle begin to worry about you, Carla?"

"My father is still weeping for the dead bitch and Luis is busy drinking and bragging with his *bandidos*. I told the sentry I wanted to spend some time with you so we could talk and I could practice my English. I also promised Juan I'd spend some time with him too."

Clint was beginning to realize there was no point in worrying about the girl's virtue when she pressed her lips against his. Carla's tongue moved artfully into his mouth and her wide, soft lips gradually increased pressure.

The Gunsmith responded to her kiss, his own tongue probing her mouth and teeth. It was difficult to believe she could be so young and kiss with such passionate skill. Clint suspected she'd already lost her virginity, but experienced or not, she was still a young girl. His hands still held the plate and chili bowl or he may have embraced her. Carla's hands, however, found his crotch and began to rub his throbbing manhood.

Clint managed to find enough space on the dirt floor to put down the food, with Carla still clinging to him, kissing and stroking at the same time. Reminding himself once again that the passionate female who was trying to work him into a sexual frenzy was a child, Clint pulled his lips from hers.

"You'd better go," he whispered, taking her hands from his trousers. The girl had already unbuttoned the fly and Clint's penis jutted from the gap like a short flagpole.

"Why?" Carla inquired. "You want me, no?"

"You're awfully young to be doing this sort of thing," he began. "I just don't feel right about it. . . ."

"You feel just fine to me," she declared, wrapping her fingers around his member, her thumb gently rubbing the sensitive head.

"No, Carla . . ." he began.

"I can scream, you know," Carla stated. "What do you think will happen if I tell Uncle Luis you tried to rape me?"

Clint's confusion, lust and apprehension had to make room for a generous chunk of anger. The little bitch was trying to blackmail him. Worse, Clint couldn't think of any way to avoid a confrontation with El Lobo except to agree to the girl's demands.

Then Carla took command of the situation once more. Her beautiful, wide mouth opened and her head sunk between Clint's legs. He felt her lips close around the head of his penis, the tip of her tongue probing and licking eagerly.

Slowly, Carla worked her lips along the length of his shaft. She used her mouth, tongue and teeth with practiced skill that rivaled any grown woman Clint had known in the past. Her ability had clearly been acquired by experience—a lot of it. How old had she been when she first began giving sexual favors? Clint found the idea of a child forced to lead such a life horribly sad.

But, even though he had done nothing to encourage her and he didn't want to, he couldn't help responding to her artful mouth. Her soft lips caressed his member and her tongue worked him like a fawn at a saltlick. Clint's manhood hardened to full length as she continued to suck his penis and slowly began to raise and lower her head.

What could Clint do? Grab the pretty little girl by the hair, yank her face from his crotch and punch her in that gorgeous mouth? His own passion was soon too aroused to want her to stop. Carla's head moved faster, her lips riding up from the root of his organ to the rim of its head.

Her hands clawed at his clothing, as her head bobbed even faster. Clint felt himself rapidly reaching the limit and he whispered her name to warn her; however, Carla ignored his words and continued to suck his hard manhood until he could no longer contain himself. Hot semen burst in the girl's mouth, but she drank him without complaint and raised her head to offer an impish grin.

"Do you still think I am too young?" she asked.

"Yes," he replied honestly.

"That's not what your body tells me, Clint," Carla stated as she rose to her feet. "Eat your dinner and regain your strength. I'll try to visit you later."

She left the *cárcel* and Clint shook his head. Poor Carla had never had a chance of a normal childhood being raised among El Lobo and his bandits. They had robbed her of more than her virginity. . . .

TWENTY-NINE

Clint managed to fall asleep after his meal. Two hours of light slumber ended abruptly when a gunshot echoed within the *bandido* camp. The Gunsmith awoke instantly, his hand nearly drawing the .22 belly gun from his shirt. Another shot erupted, followed by confused shouts in Spanish.

The shots had not been fired rapidly and Clint suspected both had come from the same weapon, a pistol, judging from the bark of the report. That meant the bandits probably weren't under attack. Clint moved to the curtain and peered out to see the *bandidos* had clustered together in the center of the hamlet. El Lobo marched toward the adobe dwellings, followed by Tomas. Guillermo walked some distance behind them, his left arm wrapped around Carla's shoulders. He had an old Colt Dragoon in his right hand. The girl appeared to be distraught and frightened, and the lesser members of the bandit gang expressed a variety of emotions— anger, disbelief, indignation. Nobody looked very happy.

Then El Lobo strode to the *cárcel* and ordered Señor Gringo to come out. Clint obeyed and asked what had happened.

"Guillermo caught Juan outside of the camp trying to rape his daughter," Mendez snorted. "Rape his daughter? *Mierda!* The fool is blind enough to believe his little slut is still a virgin angel!"

"He killed Juan?" Clint inquired, not revealing that he knew Mendez was related to the "blind fool" and the "little slut."

"*Sí,*" Mendez nodded. "The rest of my men are angry because they say they have not had a woman for weeks. How can Juan be blamed for responding to that *puta's* behavior under such circumstances? I've told them we will be in Yuma in another day or two, but they will not listen."

"Luis, *vamos a la casa* . . ." Tomas began.

"*Sí, sí!*" Mendez said angrily. "We are going to the house. That is, *you* are going, Tomas. I have two women of my own here and I don't want to leave them with the rest of these *coyotes* when they all hunger so for sex."

"You're sending your men to a cathouse?" Clint asked, finding it difficult to believe such an establishment could be found in the middle of the Arizona prairie.

"*Madre de Dios!*" Mendez rolled his eyes toward heaven. "If only one was available! After we get the gold from Manning and his *bastardos,* I think I will buy a *casa de las putas* so this will not happen in the future."

"Then what sort of house are you talking about?" Clint inquired.

"What do you care, *gringo*?" Tomas snarled.

"He should know," Mendez snapped. "I'm sending Señor Gringo with you."

"*Qué?*" Thomas gasped. "What we need him for? The Anglo will just be in the way, Luis!"

"Three reasons he goes with you, Tomas," El Lobo began. "First, we don't know how good Señor Gringo handles himself in an emergency. This way we get some idea, no? Second, I want him to be involved in a raid. After he takes part in one he'll be tied to us and won't be apt to tell the Anglo *federales* about us. And third, you'll take the *gringo* because I'm telling you do to it! *Comprende?*"

"*Si*," Tomas agreed sourly.

"Now, go get three more men to join the raiding party."

The bandit lieutenant shuffled away to carry out the command. El Lobo turned to Clint and smiled coldly. Clint wasn't sure what the *bandidos* had in mind, but he didn't think he'd care much for the explanation.

"You're sending me on a raid?" he inquired.

"A very little raid," Mendez assured him. "Do not frown so. It will not be dangerous. In fact, it is so safe, I don't even think we need to give you a gun."

"In other words," the Gunsmith sighed, "you still don't trust me with one, right?"

"Not yet, Señor Gringo," Mendez replied lightly. "Maybe later."

"What are we going to raid that'll be so easy we can do it barehanded?" Clint asked.

"Just a farmhouse about five miles from here," Mendez answered. "A scouting team we sent out to check the area found it the other day. They reported that it was a small farm with little of anything worthwhile—except for the yellow-haired woman they saw feeding chickens. In Mexico, we don't have many blonds and the scout team got all excited about her and brought back exaggerated tales of her beauty. Bah! She is probably a scrawny old vulture, but my men have been eager to get their hands on her since they heard about the farm. If we were in my country, we would have already taken the place, but small farmers in Mexico don't own guns. Here, everybody can own one.

It is much more dangerous for a *bandido* here."

"That's the American way," Clint shrugged. "The second amendment of the Constitution gives us the right to keep and bear arms. Guess the Founding Fathers didn't have much consideration for the plight you fellows might find yourselves in when they came up with that one."

Mendez smiled thinly. "I hope you're not too fond of your fellow Americans, Señor Gringo, since you'll be going with Tomas and the men he selects for the mission. None of us like Anglos very much and I think you've already noticed that Tomas likes *gringos* even less than the rest of us. You try to interfere with his raid . . . well, he won't really mind putting a bullet in you if you give him a reason, no? *Any* kind of reason."

"Yeah," Clint agreed. "And maybe I don't have to do anything except be a *gringo* to give him enough reason to kill me."

"Maybe." Mendez shrugged. "Guess you'll find out, no?"

THIRTY

Tomas led the small band, riding in front of the others with a coal-oil lantern in one hand to illuminate the path and detect prairie dog holes in the ground. Still, none of the riders attempted to urge their mounts into a gallop due to the treacherous terrain.

Clint rode a weary Morgan-mustang cross-breed without a saddle. Tomas and another *bandido* named Julio rode in front of him while the other two members of the band—Clint had heard them called as Miguel and Francisco—brought up the rear. All four *bandidos* were heavily armed with long guns, pistols and knives. Clint assumed all the hardware was to defend against a surprise Apache attack and not intended solely for the raid on a small farmhouse. Certainly, the bandits didn't feel they needed so many guns just to keep the Gunsmith in line until they reached their goal.

This mission was typical of the mentality of most outlaws and bandits, in Clint's opinion. Provided Mendez had told the truth, and Clint believed he had, they were only two days ride from a million dollars in gold. Nobody had wanted to risk riding in the night for the treasure which could make every member of the gang wealthy, but when an incident whetted their sex drive, the bandits were ready to take the very risks they'd refused before simply to have a woman for one night.

Bandits and outlaws tended to take such absurd risks for the least logical reasons. Most outlaws were just too plain dumb and lazy to try to work at an honest trade. The majority were illiterate. The Lonny Woods Gang in Omaha had actually tried to rob a library because it "sure looked like a bank" and none of the half-wits could read the sign on the building.

Outlaws were ruled by their passions for sex, strong drink and violence, and they generally wound up like El Lobo's gang—dirty, desperate men who scratched at flea bites while they waited for an opportunity to plunder their way to wealth.

However, even if Tomas and the other three men signed their names with an X and had to open their trousers to count to eleven, none of them would hesitate to blow Clint's head off for half a reason, and they were all better armed than the Gunsmith. The odds were still in the bandits' favor, but now Clint only had to deal with four men instead of the entire gang and none of them knew about his belly gun.

Clint would have to wait for a chance to get the bandits off guard. There was no question about returning to the camp. No better opportunity was apt to come along for him to escape from the gang and he damn sure didn't relish riding into Yuma with them. He had enough trouble trying to live with his reputation as the Gunsmith let alone trying to explain how he'd wound up with a pack of Mexican hootowls.

At last they saw the farm. It was a simple little spread with a few hundred acres of wheat or barley, Clint couldn't tell which in the darkness. There was a small one-story house and a slightly larger barn with a corral extending from one side and a chicken coop at the other.

Tomas extinguished the lantern and dismounted. He

whispered some orders to his men and they quickly ground hobbled the horses. Clint followed their example. The *bandido* lieutenant drew one of his three revolvers and explained his strategy to the men and then turned to the Gunsmith.

"You listen close, *gringo*," Tomas demanded. "Miguel and Julio are going to approach the house at the front door. Francisco will go around to the side and cover the window there. Me and you go to the back door. You do exactly what I tell you or I kill you. *¿Comprende?*"

"I think I can manage to follow your instructions, Tomas . . . er, *teniente*," Clint replied.

The group moved forward on foot, quickly covering the three hundred or so yards between where they'd hobbled the horses and the farmhouse. Clint half expected to hear a dog bark an alert followed by rifle shots from the farmhouse. Luckily for the raiding party, Clint included, the farm didn't seem to have a watchdog on duty and there was no activity from the house.

They closed in swiftly, boots hammering the ground without any attempt at stealth. Everybody inside the house—if there was anyone inside—had to be sleeping like a pile of woodchips. Clint had always wondered about the type of people who'd set up a tiny little spread in an area surrounded by hostile Indians, often miles away from their nearest neighbors. If this was an example of the kinds of precautions they took against possible assaults, Clint considered it amazing that they hadn't been wiped out long ago.

Miguel and Julio hurried to the front of the house while Francisco took his position at the side window. Clint and Tomas moved to the rear entrance. The bandit's face was aglow with anticipation as he dragged the revolver from his other hip holster and held both guns ready.

"I'm gonna fire a shot to signal the attack," he whispered to Clint. "Then you just stand back and let us take care of everything."

"You're just going to gun down everybody in that house?" Clint inquired, reaching inside his shirt.

"Except the women," Tomas shrugged.

"What if there are children in there?" Clint asked. "Or old people?"

"If the girls aren't too young or the women too old we take them," Tomas replied. "Otherwise they get a bullet."

Clint cocked the hammer of his New Line Colt as he pointed it at Tomas's face.

"You first, *teniente*," the Gunsmith informed him. "Drop your guns."

Tomas whirled, trying to train the revolvers on Clint. The New Line barked twice and the *bandido's* head snapped back as two .22 bullets drilled into it. He was dead before he could cock the hammer of either gun in his fists.

Moving with uncanny speed, Clint tossed the New Line from his right hand to his left and caught it as he lunged forward. He quickly yanked the third revolver from Tomas's belt—an S&W .44—before the dead man could fall to the ground. Then he pivoted and kicked the door open.

Miguel and Julio broke through the front door a split second later. The Gunsmith and the bandits stood at opposite sides of an unlit room, facing each other—three vague shapes in the shadows.

Clint didn't hesitate. He couldn't afford to. The S&W in his right hand and the Colt in his left snarled. A .22 bullet hit Miguel high in the chest and a .44 drilled into Julio's heart. The muzzle flash of the weapons lit up the room in an orange glare for an instant, long enough for Clint to see Julio was dead, but Miguel only wounded.

He swung the S&W toward Miguel and tried to squeeze the trigger. Nothing happened. Accustomed to years of using his converted Colt double-action model in a gunfight that required rapid fire, Clint had failed to cock the hammer of the unfamiliar single-action pistol.

Miguel's pistol snapped off a shot at Clint, the bullet tearing splinters from the door frame behind the Gunsmith. Clint thumbed back the S&W hammer and blasted another round into the *bandido's* chest. This time Miguel went down for good.

Glass shattered to Clint's right as Francisco shoved the twin barrels of a Stevens shotgun through the window at the side of the house. Clint hadn't forgotten about the last member of the team. He'd already turned to face the window and fired his pistols before Francisco could use his formidable weapon.

A .44 and a .22 punched through the windowpane and did the same to Francisco's face. As the *bandido* fell backward, he raised the shotgun and a muscle reaction pulled a trigger. The Stevens bellowed, blasting a load of buckshot into the ceiling. Then the gun barrels disappeared out the window to join Francisco's corpse on the ground outside.

Clint managed to locate a table in the center of the dark room and placed both the New Line and the S&W on it. He began to raise his hands and was surprised to find they were trembling a bit. The Gunsmith was no stranger to the effects of tension following a gunfight, but he hadn't had the shakes after such a conflict for years.

His stomach was still knotted up as well and his knees felt weak. The effects were more dramatic than they should have been for a professional with Clint's experience. He felt almost as badly shaken as he had been as a kid when he'd first killed a man in a gunfight.

"Hold it!" a woman's voice ordered. "You just keep your hands high or I'll shoot you dead right where you stand!"

"I put my guns on the table, ma'am," Clint told her. "I'm about to light the lamp here so you'll see the men I just killed who'd broken into your home."

"The lamp?" the woman's voice expressed horror. "No! Don't!"

But Clint had already struck a match and held it to the wick of the coal-oil lamp on the table. The room was instantly bathed in yellow light. Clint saw the cause of the woman's consternation. She was stark naked.

A tall blond with long hair and a beautifully sculptured pair of pink-tipped breasts, she stood at the entrance of a bedroom with an old Henry carbine in her hands. The woman's flat belly extended to flared hips and long tapered legs with a golden triangle between the thighs. Her lovely face was contorted by embarrassment and confusion that was almost on the brink of panic. She tried to alter the angle of the Henry to use it to somehow cover her nude body.

"Uh . . ." she began awkwardly. "What do you want?"

"You really shouldn't ask that question until you put some clothes on, ma'am."

THIRTY-ONE

While the woman retreated into her bedroom, Clint relieved the bodies of Miguel and Julio of their firearms and gunbelts. Then he dragged them out the back door and laid them beside the corpse of *Teniente* Tomas. After stripping Tomas of his gunbelt and picking up the dead man's fallen pistols, Clint moved to the side of the house and prepared to add Francisco's body to the collection. Clint gathered up the bandit's shotgun and examined it as best he could under the night sky, which was too dark to make a valid inspection possible.

However, an idea had already formed in Clint's head. He searched Francisco's body and found a leather pouch full of shotgun shells. The Gunsmith decided to leave the body be for now and re-entered the house with the shotgun in one hand and the other items cradled in his other arm.

The blond had emerged from her bedroom dressed in a quilted robe. She seemed a bit apprehensive when Clint entered with his arms loaded up with weapons, but she wasn't holding a gun and didn't seem to feel she'd need one. Clint smiled weakly at her. When he was cleaned up, he was a pleasant-looking man whom many women found attractive despite the scar on his left cheek. However, he still wore the same filthy denim shirt and trousers and mud clung to his hair. The Gunsmith's face had been burned by hours of exposure without a hat to the merciless Arizona sun. He could only guess what the poor woman thought of him, seeing him in such condition.

"I'm sorry about my appearance, ma'am," he began, a bit sheepishly. "And I'm even more sorry that I had to resort to violence here in your home. If you'd be willing to let me explain, I'll be glad to do so, but it'll take a while. Sort of a long story and I'm not sure about some parts myself."

The woman just stared at Clint.

"Maybe, it'd be best if I just move on—" he began.

"No!" she said sharply. "Don't be silly. You probably saved my life and . . . well, I would like to hear your story, Mister . . . ?"

"Adams," he smiled. "But please call me Clint."

"I'm Jenny Parker," she stated. "Uh, maybe I should fix some coffee, Clint."

"That sounds fine," the Gunsmith readily agreed. "And if you can spare enough water, I'd really appreciate . . ."

"Oh! Of course!" Jenny replied. "There's a well outside and a bucket. If you'll just haul in the water, I'll heat it up for you and we'll fill the tub."

An hour later, Clint felt as if he'd found paradise. His long legs were doubled up to allow his body to soak in the hot bath water as he scrubbed the filth and stink from his flesh and hair. The lye-based soap was a bit harsh on his sunburned face, but that was a small sacrifice for the relief the hot water brought to his stiff, sore muscles.

The tub was located at the back of the house with a wooden screen around it for privacy. Clint had placed a chair near the tub with the S&W on the seat, just in case Apaches or El Lobo's people made an unexpected visit.

He didn't think either was likely, especially the latter. Luis Mendez was too hardhearted and practical to send out a search party after the first team failed to return. He'd write them off like an accountant checking expenses for an Eastern law firm and use them as an example to the rest of his men not to wander around in hostile Indian territory after dark.

At sunrise, Mendez and the remnants of his gang would move on to Yuma. Clint hoped Guillermo and Carla wouldn't go with the *bandidos*. Maybe if the sad-faced man broke off connections with his brother, he might be able to start over somewhere else and give Carla a chance to be something more than a bandit's plaything or a whore.

The bath was wonderful. It seemed to soak out Clint's tension as well as the grime and dirt. Relaxing in the warm water, he was able to put together a plan concerning his own actions after he left the Parker farm at dawn. He still had to move on to Yuma and see to Duke and his wagon—and hopefully to settle a couple scores with Lloyd and the others.

Someone moved toward the wooden screen and Clint reached for the pistol before he saw Jenny slip into the compartment. She carried a blue tin mug of coffee in one hand and a pair of Levis and a checkered shirt in the other.

"Sorry to disturb your bath," she said with a smile in her voice. "But I figured you might like some coffee now."

"Jenny, you're an angel," Clint replied. He started to move forward a bit in the tub, but then decided he'd better not.

"You got to see me without any clothes on so I didn't think you'd be so shy."

"My upbringing, ma'am," Clint answered. "Where'd you get the clothes?"

"They belonged to my husband," Jenny said. "He died four months ago."

"I'm sorry, Jenny," Clint told her. "You shouldn't stay out here by yourself. What happened tonight should convince you of that."

"What exactly did happen tonight, Clint?" she asked. "How'd you get mixed up with those Mexican killers?"

"That's a long story," Clint sighed. "It started in Brownsville, Texas and I'm hoping it'll end in Yuma pretty soon. This is sort of an awkward way to have a conversation. Can we talk after I finish my bath?"

"Sure," she said. "Oh, there's a hole in this shirt. I'll just take it inside and sew it for you while you finish cleaning up."

"Thanks, Jenny," the Gunsmith told her. "I can't tell you how much I appreciate all this."

"Nonsense," the woman replied. "You saved my life, didn't you?"

Jenny took the checkered shirt and headed back into the house. Clint decided he'd soaked long enough and climbed out of the tub to towel himself dry. The water in the tub looked as if it had been scooped out of a swamp with all the filth he'd scrubbed off his body. Clint was grateful he had a clean pair of trousers to climb into after finally ridding himself of all that dirt and mud. The pants were a bit loose at the waist and the cuffs were an inch too short, but otherwise they fit pretty well.

Bare-chested and barefooted, he padded back inside the house with the S&W in hand. He entered the kitchen, surprised that Jenny wasn't seated at the table.

"I'm in here, Clint," the woman's voice called from the bedroom.

The Gunsmith followed it and found Jenny seated on the bed. Even in the shadows of the unlit bedroom, Clint saw the pale flesh displayed by her open housecoat.

"Come in," she said softly.

Clint placed his cup on the kitchen table before heading for the bedroom. As he approached, Jenny rose from the bed and shrugged off her robe. Clint found a nightstand by the bed and put the S&W revolver on it.

"Do you think you'll need a gun in here?" Jenny inquired, amusement in her tone.

"Not unless we get interrupted," Clint answered.

He turned to face her. Jenny's arms snaked around his neck and Clint leaned forward to place his lips against her's. His arms encircled her waist, hands stroking the smooth, soft flesh. They kissed and embraced tenderly, savoring the feel of flesh on flesh and warm lips pressed together. Tongues probed gently and their hands gradually caressed bare skin.

Clint would have guessed he'd been too worn out to respond to such an invitation. He'd endured a lot of physical abuse and had little rest over the last twenty-four hours. Carla's visit in the *bandido* prison cell must have drained him of any sexual stamina he could possibly have had left after his grueling ordeal—or so Clint would have guessed.

Jenny stroked his erection slowly, unbuttoning his trousers to free his member. Her hands gently played with his penis, using only the fingertips, stimulating his throbbing manhood with her touch. Many women will merely take a man in their fists and pound away until his teeth are clenched and he's wondering what he'd said or done to deserve such torment. Jenny, however, treated Clint to gradual, loving strokes that soon had his organ jutting out, hard and ready.

The Gunsmith cupped Jenny's firm, round breasts in his hands. He'd never been one to manhandle a woman and he gently caressed her, kissing each breast slowly and tracing his tongue around the nipples until he felt them stiffen between his lips. Clint sucked her breasts, teasing the hard pink nipples with his teeth.

Clint released Jenny and slid down his trousers. Totally nude, he stepped out of them and prepared to steer Jenny toward the bed. However, the girl closed a hand around his erect member and pulled gently. She guided him to the bed, clearly a silent request for him to lie down first.

Clint obliged, stretching out on the mattress, the back of his head sinking into a soft, feather-filled pillow. Jenny climbed onto the bed, her hands stroking Clint's chest and belly. Then her mouth worked its way along his bare flesh, kissing and licking his freshly washed skin, her long blond hair sliding over him like a velvet sash.

Jenny's mouth found his crotch, but she didn't linger there. She once again applied her gentle, magic touch, stroking his erection and tenderly fondling his testicles. Then she slid a leg over his loins and eased herself into position.

Clint felt himself enter the woman. Jenny felt like a warm, wet towel surrounded by muscle. She clung firmly to his manhood, engulfing it in her love cave. Her knees and thighs pressed against his hips as she slowly began to raise and lower herself upon his member.

Jenny slid up and down Clint's manhood as his hands found her breasts and again began to fondle the soft mounds. He felt them bounce in his grasp as Jenny increased the momentum of her body. She moaned with pleasure as she continued to ride. Clint's heels pressed into the mattress as he arched his back to thrust deeply into Jenny. The bed creaked and seemed about to rise from the floor as Jenny and Clint continued in their vigorous lovemaking.

The girl gasped and thrashed her head from side to

side as an orgasm swept through her. Clint could no longer deny his own sensual release and came seconds later. Jenny raked his chest with her nails and hummed with pleasure, feeling his throbbing shaft within her.

"Oh, God," she whispered breathlessly. "You are good."

"So are you," Clint assured her.

"I hope you don't think I'd do this sort of thing with just any stranger who happened by," Jenny remarked, slowly dismounting from his crotch to sprawl beside him.

Although exhausted, Clint took her in his arms and kissed her, holding Jenny tenderly. He had never been a selfish lover and the fulfillment of his partner was as important to Clint as his own satisfaction. The Gunsmith understood women better than most men and he knew they like to be cuddled and held after making love.

"Of course I don't," Clint assured her, aware that women are afraid a man will consider them whorish for simply having a normal sex drive.

"Who are you, Clint Adams?" she asked, trying to read his face in the darkness. "You handle a gun well enough to take four Mexican bandits, yet you're polite and well-bred and you surely know how to treat a woman."

"I'm just Clint Adams," the Gunsmith told her. "And I'm going to have to move on in the morning. You know that, don't you?"

"Why do you think I wanted to do this tonight?" she replied softly, taking his soft member in her magical hands.

He was about to protest, but was surprised to find himself growing hard again. Soon it felt too good to want her to stop.

"You never did tell me that story of yours," Jenny remarked.

"Are you sure you want to hear it now?" he asked.

"I'm sure," she stated, still stroking him as she spoke.

The Gunsmith told her about being hired in Brownsville and briefly explained the events on the train and how he fell in with El Lobo's gang. He didn't bother to mention any of his sexual exploits with any of the women involved.

He frequently halted in his narrative to kiss her neck or nibble on an ear lobe or nipple and his hands caressed her flesh throughout the story. By the time he'd finished his tale, they were both ready to make love a second time.

Clint mounted her and Jenny eagerly took him in. He began to grind his hips, hearing her moan in sensual approval. Jenny's long, strong legs wrapped around his waist and pulled him closer, encouraging Clint to ram himself home. Naturally, he responded and brought the woman to another gasping, trembling orgasm. Clint rode her to paradise a third time before he blasted his seed inside Jenny's beautiful, lusty body.

"You sure know how to please a lady," she commented in a sleepy voice.

Clint kissed her in response and soon they were sound asleep, still holding each other in a lovers' embrace.

THIRTY-TWO

The smell of coffee brewing and eggs and bacon frying in skillets greeted the Gunsmith when he awoke. Jenny Parker was busy in the kitchen, singing softly as she prepared breakfast. Clint forced himself to rise from the comfort of the nice warm bed.

He slowly stretched and discovered most of the soreness in his muscles had disappeared. Clint pulled on the Levis and located the checkered shirt. As he slipped into the shirt and buttoned it Clint smiled, recalling the night before. He shuffled from the bedroom to find Jenny setting the table.

"Figured you'd be up when you got a whiff of breakfast," Jenny said brightly. "How do you feel today, Clint?"

"A lot better than I have for quite a while," he replied. "Any idea what time it is?"

"Sun came up about an hour ago," Jenny answered. "You've got time for breakfast. Just sit down and eat before you go riding off after those badmen."

"Ride," Clint said. "I'd better see to those horses the bandits left outside."

"They'll keep," Jenny told him.

Clint shook his head. "Those animals ought to be fed and watered. Not their fault they belonged to El Lobo's men. Besides, I'll have to look them over and pick the best mount of the lot."

Jenny sighed, but didn't argue. Clint found his boots
sitting by the door. Jenny had brushed off most of the
mud and given them a coat of saddle soap. He smiled
with appreciation and pulled on the footgear.

Clint found the horses where the *bandidos* had left
them. The animals were accustomed to the rough treat-
ment of their bandit owners and appeared no worse for
wear after spending several hours hobbled outside. The
Gunsmith led them by the reins to the barn and tended
to the beasts. Tomas's mount, a big Appaloosa stallion,
was easily the best horse of the lot.

He then selected the best saddle, checking the straps
for signs of wear and the leather for cracks. Then he returned to the house and had breakfast with Jenny. Clint
complimented her on the meal, which indeed deserved
his praise. Then he excused himself from the table.

Clint rose from his chair and moved to the pile of firearms he'd taken from the bandits. The Gunsmith examined each pistol carefully and soon narrowed his selec-
tion down to two .45 Colt models. He opened the load-
ing gate of one revolver and shook out the shells one by
one.

"What are you doing, Clint?" Jenny asked, confused
by his actions.

"Trying to decide which gun to carry until I get my
own back," he replied. "That Smith & Wesson I used
last night is a good enough gun, but I'm not used to the
model. I had trouble getting shots off fast enough. I
need something similar to the revolver I'm familiar
with." He didn't bother to explain his problem in detail.
Only a fellow shootist could understand how serious his
situation was.

For a man to be good with a gun, really *good,* he had
to have a feel for the weapon. He needed to be familiar
with it. Whether or not the barrel tended to pull to any

particular direction when it fired a round, the shape of the grips, trigger pull, width of the hammer—all were crucial. In Clint's case, this presented an even worse obstacle since he was accustomed to a one-of-a-kind gun.

For the first time, his skill with the modified Colt had become a liability. He now understood why he'd had the shakes after the gun battle with the *bandidos*—because he could no longer be confident in his own ability. He'd nearly been killed because he'd tried to use a single-action revolver as he would his double-action Colt.

Clint disassembled the *bandido* pistols and checked the condition of the guns. One revolver had a worn trigger lever and a pitted barrel. The other was in excellent condition. He wondered which bandit had owned the gun, but it was really a moot point now.

Then he checked the confiscated gunbelts, ignoring Tomas's rig with its twin holsters. Clint settled for a single holster gunbelt which would suit his build. The *bandido* gunbelt wasn't a quick-draw rig, but it wouldn't make any difference if Clint came up against a man like Stansfield Lloyd.

The Gunsmith would be killed.

However, Clint had a plan to help compensate for the loss of his converted Colt. It would require the modification of a firearm, but a much less complex job than turning a single-action revolver into a double-action weapon.

"Did your husband have any tools in the barn, Jenny?" he inquired, reaching for the Stevens shotgun that had formerly belonged to Francisco.

"Uh . . . yes," she replied awkwardly.

"Mind if I use them to do a little work on this shotgun?"

"Help yourself," Jenny replied with a curious stare.

Clint carried the Stevens to the barn and, to his delight, found a small blacksmith forge with an assortment of tools for working with metal as well as wood. He was surprised to discover the tools had recently been oiled and cleaned, but he didn't question good fortune.

A work bench with a large vice provided a solid clamp for the shotgun. He tightened the vice around the barrels at the forestock and applied a hacksaw to the Stevens. One item that wasn't available was a piece of chalk to mark the barrel for a clean cut, but Clint kept the saw steady and didn't rush the job. Slowly, he hacked through the thick barrels, slicing roughly two inches above the forestock.

When Clint had sawed off most of the Stevens' barrels, he used a heavy metal file to scrape down the rough edges at the muzzles of the abbreviated shotgun. A perfectionist when it came to firearms, horses and making love, the Gunsmith took his time with the file until the barrels met with his approval.

Adjusting the vice to clamp the butt stock, Clint then took a wood saw to the Stevens, cutting the hard walnut just behind the pistol grips of the shotgun. When the bulk of the butt stock had been removed, Clint found some sandpaper and carefully smoothed down the back of the pistol grips.

"You're gonna be just fine," he assured the shotgun as he fussed over it some more.

He oiled the metal, cleaned the barrels and applied a light coat of varnish to the shortened stock. Then, at last, it was complete.

A scattergun.

The short barrels would reduce the range drastically. Maximum practical range would be less than a dozen feet, preferably about half that distance. But at close quarters, the scattergun would be unbeatable against two opponents or more if they bunched together. The pattern of buckshot from a scattergun spreads like a hand-thrown net.

Due to the short barrels and abbreviated stock, the gun would kick like a deranged jackass and there'd be no real accuracy, but there didn't have to be. Just point it and squeeze the trigger. The buckshot would do the rest. The weapon only had two real drawbacks. It would only hold two shells at a time and it was an indiscriminate weapon that couldn't be used if innocent bystanders were close at hand.

The first problem was compensated for by the devastating potential of a buckshot blast and the fact that the shotgun could be reloaded rapidly. Clint would simply have to use good judgment to deal with the latter problem, but he always exercised care and proper safety with any type of firearm. No gun ever harmed anyone without human assistance, either by intentional action or by mishandling the weapon. Clint had never shot anyone by accident and if he took a gun out of leather, he fully intended to use it.

Leather. Clint hunted about the barn workshop until he located a large piece of tanned leather, knives, needles and catgut. He wasn't as familiar with working with leather as he was with guns, but he'd made functional holsters before and what he needed was simple enough. After cutting and sewing for less than half an hour, he'd accomplished the task.

The shotgun holster was little more than a wide strip of leather attached to his gunbelt in a cross-draw position, but it would allow him to carry the Stevens on his person at all times. His work finished, Clint cleaned up the workshop and left the barn.

Jenny stared at him in astonishment as he led the Appaloosa from the corral, her eyes locked on the modified Stevens in the crude holster at his waist. She whistled softly.

"When you go after somebody, you don't take any chances," she remarked.

"I'm only going after what's rightfully mine," the Gunsmith explained. "But I doubt that I'll be able to get it back peaceably and that means I can't afford to take any more chances than I have to."

"I guess you're doing what you have to, Clint," she nodded. "Better just say good-bye and have done with it."

"The bandit's horses, guns and leather goods will be worth some money, Jenny," Clint told her gently. "More than enough to pay for the damage to your house."

"Don't fret about that," she urged.

"But I am concerned about you," Clint insisted. "You shouldn't be out here all alone. You can sell the farm and move into a town. Maybe Yuma—"

"Yuma is where you're headed, Clint," she stated. "It's right that way to the west. Keep going the way I told you and I bet you'll be there before those bandits arrive, even if they did leave at dawn. . . ."

"I have to bury those four dead men, Jenny," he declared grimly.

"Those bodies will keep," Jenny said. "They aren't going anywhere."

"Don't be absurd," Clint sighed. It was obvious she wanted him to leave quickly. Did she want to get the farewells over to lessen the pain of parting? Was she afraid if he stayed any longer she'd break down and beg him not to go?

"Damn it, Clint!" Jenny snapped. "My husband will take care of burying those bodies when he gets home in about three hours."

The Gunsmith stared at her. "Your husband? But you said—"

"He was dead," she nodded. "Well, he isn't. He's in

Yuma selling barley to a saloon that brews it into beer."

Clint shook his head as though trying to recover from a physical blow. "Why, Jenny?"

"I lied to you so we could sleep together." She shrugged. "A woman's got needs, you know. Arnold is a good husband, but he hasn't satisfied me much in bed these days."

The Gunsmith grinned, not in amusement, but irony. He'd been worried about Jenny, but she'd be all right . . . providing her husband didn't find out how she'd entertained her houseguest. He swung up into the saddle.

"Thanks for everything," he told her. "Good luck."

"Good luck to you, Clint," Jenny replied. "I've got a feeling you'll need it."

"Can't argue with you about that," he admitted.

THIRTY-THREE

Clint Adams arrived in Yuma later that afternoon. Due to its proximity to Fort Yuma, the city had attracted a fairly large population since many people preferred to be close to the cavalry in the Arizona Territory. The Chiricahua Apaches under Cochise had made a truce with the army, but everyone suspected it was just a matter of time before someone—white or red—with a chip on his shoulder would start the whole mess up again. Besides, the truce only applied to the Chiricahua. The dozen or so smaller Apache tribes hadn't seen fit to make peace with the white eyes.

Yuma had a large number of businesses, many designed to appeal to the cavalrymen who made excursions into town whenever the fort commander gave them leave. Locating the train station was easy enough since the railroad tracks extended along that end of Yuma. The Gunsmith felt anticipation rise in his chest when he saw the train had just arrived.

Clint approached the locomotive at a gradual pace, allowing his horse to trot toward it. He wasn't worried that Lloyd, Linda or Vargas would recognize him from a distance since his face and hands had been tanned brown by the sun and he wore a straw sombrero, confiscated from a slain *bandido,* with the broad brim pulled

161

low over his upper face. The only article of clothing he wore that he hadn't acquired at the Parker farm were his boots. Clint's horse, saddle and weapons wouldn't betray his identity either.

As Clint drew closer, he recognized Andrew Waitley, the conductor, who stood at the engine compartment talking to one of the engineers. Clint steered the Appaloosa toward the head of the train. Waitley and the engineer looked at him with irritation, wondering what this Mexican in Anglo clothing wanted.

The Gunsmith dismounted and strode to the engine. "Hello, Mr. Waitley," he greeted, cocking back the brim of his sombrero with a thumb.

"Mr. Adams?" the conductor asked, still not certain.

"That's right," Clint nodded.

"What are you doing dressed like that?" Waitley asked, and then introduced Clint to the engineer, Mike Randall, explaining that Adams had been on the train. "Mr. Lloyd told us you were going to ride on to Yuma, but I don't remember seeing you get off the train. I know you didn't leave when the rest of your crew got off so—"

"Hold on," Clint urged. "You mean Lloyd and Vargas and dear Miss Mather got off the train *before* it reached Yuma?"

"You weren't aware of that?" Waitley asked as though he suspected Clint might be retarded.

"You might say they dropped me off a couple days ago," the Gunsmith replied dryly. "I haven't been on the train for almost forty-eight hours, but since nobody seemed to notice when Detective Patterson disappeared, I'm not surprised no one knew I'd been thrown off the train."

"Thrown off!" both his listeners exclaimed.

"Never mind that," Clint stated. "Tell me about

Lloyd and the others. When did they get off?"

"About two hours ago we come across this wagon smack dab in the middle of the tracks," the engineer explained. "There was one feller sitting in the rig and a couple others standin' by it. All of them were waving at us to stop. Well, I figured they might need help or they could be outlaws settin' up a trap, but I stopped anyway."

"Then Mister Lloyd informs me he and the rest of his party—or at least *most* of them—were getting off right there and then," Waitley added. "Well, this was very unusual, but frankly, we were glad to be rid of him, that Vargas character and that troublesome woman . . . not that we had the same attitude about you, Mr. Adams! Well, everything that belonged to Miss Mather was unloaded and they put it on that wagon. Obviously they expected to meet those men, but why they didn't want to travel all the way to Yuma completely baffles me."

"Two hours ago." Clint frowned. "About how far back do you figure this happened?"

"Oh, twelve, fifteen miles, I reckon," the engineer answered. "If you was to—"

Suddenly, the engineer stopped talking and stared at something behind Clint. Waitley's face also expressed surprise and alarm at whatever he saw beyond the Gunsmith. The hairs on the back of Clint's neck stood at attention and his hand moved to the pistol grips of his holstered Stevens sawed-off.

"*Buenas días*, Señor Gringo," a familiar voice growled.

Clint pivoted, drawing the scattergun and thumbing back a hammer in a single fluid motion. Luis Mendez stood with a pistol aimed at Clint's head, thumb still easing back the hammer. El Lobo's face turned from a savage mask of fury to a pale etching of terror when he suddenly found himself staring into the twin muzzles of the sawed-off shotgun.

Then Mendez could no longer display expressions on his face because he lost it forever when Clint squeezed the trigger of his Stevens. A blast of buckshot literally tore El Lobo's head from his shoulders.

Clint scrambled inside the engine compartment, barely glancing at the other *bandidos* who surrounded the decapitated corpse of their leader. The bandits were stunned and horrified by the unexpected and ghastly death of their *jefe,* but they hesitated less than a second before dragging pistols from holsters and swinging rifle muzzles toward the Gunsmith.

One of the riflemen began to point a Winchester at Clint. The second barrel of the shotgun roared and the *bandido* was turned into a flying chunk of bloodied meat. Clint grabbed Waitley with his left hand and shoved him into Mike, throwing both men off balance.

They hit the floor of the engine compartment just in time. A volley of bullets clanged and whined as projectiles ricocheted off the iron structure. Clint told the conductor and engineer to stay down, then he quickly crawled to the opposite side of the engine.

As he'd suspected, the bandits had tried to surround the train engine to launch a two-prong attack. Two of El Lobo's human wolves were creeping around the front of the cowcatcher toward the compartment. Clint drew his Colt and cocked the revolver as he aimed at the closest man's chest. The *bandido* saw him a second before Clint squeezed the trigger. His cry of "*¡Mierda!*" was the last word he'd ever utter.

The other bandit retreated to the shelter of the cowcatcher, snapping off a hasty round at the Gunsmith which whined off the metal frame of the engine. Clint located the brake lever and shoved it forward. The train slowly began to roll. The bandit or bandits in front of the train would be forced to move out of the way and they wouldn't hop in the direction that the Gunsmith had just fired.

Clint guessed they'd try another assault from their original position and scrambled across the compartment, nearly trampling Waitley and Randall. He saw two bandits about to open fire at the interior of the engine. One had a pistol, the other a rifle. Clint picked off the rifleman with a .45 round through the forehead. The other man dashed for cover along the length of the train cars.

"Cover this position," Clint ordered, extending the Colt, butt first, to Mike. "Don't shoot anyone unless you're sure of the target. If you can't get a clear shot at a bandit, fire at the ground so you don't hit an innocent bystander."

The engineer took the pistol and nodded woodenly at the Gunsmith. Clint immediately broke open his shotgun and dumped out the spent shell casings. Then he shoved in two fresh 12-gauge cartridges and closed the Stevens even as he headed once again to the opposite side of the engine.

After glancing about to be certain it was relatively safe, he hopped off the slowly moving train. Clint jogged to the closest boxcar and grabbed the iron rungs of a ladder built onto its side. He climbed the rungs to the roof, wondering how many of the *bandido* gang were left to deal with. He doubted that Guillermo, Carla or either of El Lobo's women would be involved in the fight. That meant there couldn't be more than four left—unless Mendez had gotten reinforcements between the Pueblo hamlet and Yuma, which didn't seem likely.

Clint reached the roof and rolled onto the top. He

stayed low as he glanced over the edge to see two bandits trying to shuffle along beside the moving engine, using it for cover while staying away from the line of fire from the compartment. Then something drew Clint's attention out of the corner of his eye. He peered down at the gap between the boxcar and the engine compartment to see another bandit had climbed onto the coupling linking the two together.

The Gunsmith gripped the rim of the roof with his left hand and dug in as best he could with the toes of his boots to anchor himself as he leaned forward and raised the Stevens in his right hand.

"Amigo?" he said softly.

The bandit on the coupling turned and raised his head to look up at the speaker. Clint swung the shotgun, smacking the heavy barrels into the *bandido's* upturned face. The blow knocked the fellow from the train. He tumbled across the ground and lay unconscious with blood seeping from a mashed in nose and two split lips.

Suddenly, the report of a pistol accompanied the violent snapping of wood as a bullet bit into the roof an inch from Clint's right side. He shoved hard, rolling to the left and bringing the shotgun around to point it at the *bandido* who'd managed to climb onto the roof. Later, Clint would guess the man had scaled a ladder to another boxcar and worked his way to the Gunsmith's position.

Right then, Clint didn't care if the son of a bitch had been fired from a slingshot and landed on the roof with him. The Mexican outlaw cocked his revolver at the same moment the Gunsmith thumbed back one of the shotgun hammers. Clint squeezed a trigger and the Stevens roared before the *bandido* could open fire. Buckshot blew the fellow off the roof like a tremendous gust of wind. One moment he was there and the next, he was gone.

The shots from the roof attracted the attention of the two bandits stationed at the engine. They fired pistols up at the Gunsmith, splintering wood at the lip of the roof. However, Clint stayed low and none of their bullets came close to his position. The bandits broke cover, forgetting that the train was moving and the engineer and conductor were still inside the engine compartment.

The crack of the Colt Clint had given to Mike mingled with the bandits' shots. One of the hootowls from south of the border went down with two bullets in his stomach. The other turned and fired at the engine compartment. When Clint heard the metallic whine of bullets striking iron, he ventured a peek and saw the lone *bandido* firing at Mike and Waitley.

The Gunsmith aimed his shotgun at the last member of El Lobo's gang and squeezed the trigger. The bandit's upper torso seemed to transform into freshly ground beef. The force of the buckshot blast hurtled the man five feet and he crashed to the dust, too dead to even manage a decent twitch.

The engineer yanked the brake and the train came to a halt, having moved less than two yards since the battle began. Clint reloaded his Stevens although it appeared the fight was over. A crowd began to form around the train. Voices expressed horror when they saw the grisly display of the effects of buckshot on human flesh.

"So don't stand around and stare at it," Clint muttered with disgust.

Soon the local sheriff and three deputies pushed their way through the crowd. Clint climbed down from the boxcar. The sheriff eyed the Gunsmith with suspicion, especially when he saw the shotgun in the belly holster.

"You get your hands high, mister," the lawman

snapped. "You got some mighty big explainin' to do!"

"It's a long story, Sheriff," Clint sighed wearily, raising his hands overhead. "And getting longer all the time."

THIRTY-FOUR

"I've heard about you, Mr. Adams," Sheriff Neil Krammer declared after he'd listened to Clint's story.

"Call me Clint," the Gunsmith urged. He sat in the lawman's office, his shotgun and Colt .45 on the sheriff's desk.

"All right, Clint," Krammer nodded. "You know you're lucky the conductor and engineer backed up your story or you might have had a heap of trouble explaining that gunfight with those Mexicans."

"Would you have thought I'd start a fight with eight men, Sheriff?" Clint asked dryly.

"Not hardly," Krammer admitted. "I might not have believed you were really the Gunsmith if you hadn't taken 'em, though. I never heard of you using a scatter-gun or wearin' a Mex sombrero before."

"I had to improvise," Clint explained.

"Way I heard it," Krammer began, taking out a tobacco pouch and rolling papers, "you usually travel around in your gunsmith wagon or ride a big black Arabian that's suppose to be the most beautiful horse this side of Kentucky."

"Duke and my wagon are still on the train, Sheriff," Clint replied. "I'd like to reclaim them now, if you don't have any more questions for me."

"Sure enough," the sheriff agreed, gesturing at the

pistol and shotgun on his desk. "May as well take those too."

"Thanks," Clint said, gathering up his weapons and returning them to their holsters.

"From what I've heard about you," Krammer commented as he finished building a cigarette, "you favor a six-gun. Why the sawed-off?"

"A pistol has to be specially made for a fast draw and rapid, accurate shooting," Clint explained. "I'm just not used to a single-action Colt."

"That shotgun is too big and heavy to quick draw with," the lawman stated, lighting his cigarette. "Even I know that much. You don't plan to just gun this Lloyd feller down without givin' him a fair chance, do you?"

"No," Clint assured him. "I just don't intend to give *myself* less than a fair chance."

"Well, I've heard about Lloyd too," Krammer said, donning his stetson. "He's suppose to be quick as a snake and just as deadly. Hope you know what you're doing, Clint."

"Me too, Sheriff," the Gunsmith admitted.

"Mind if I tag along and watch you unload your property off the train? I've heard so much about you, I'm kinda curious to see that wagon and horse."

"If you can stand the excitement, Sheriff," Clint grinned.

"Figure we both had enough excitement for one day."

The Gunsmith and Sheriff Krammer walked to the train station and watched the railroad personnel roll Clint's wagon out of a freight car. Krammer inspected the rig with interest while Clint led Duke out of a cattle car, whispering gently to the animal, assuring him that everything was all right now.

Krammer stared at the big, black gelding as Clint

brushed soot and grime from Duke's glossy coat. Although the Arabian was dirty and his stride was a bit unsteady after two days of being cooped up in a train car, Duke was still the most magnificent horse the lawman had ever seen.

"God, he's a beauty," Krammer sighed. "If I had enough money . . ."

"I wouldn't sell Duke for any price," Clint told him, patting the horse's muzzle. "We've been partners too long to split up now."

"Partners?" Krammer raised his eyebrows with surprise. He obviously couldn't understand what Clint felt for Duke, so the Gunsmith didn't bother trying to explain it.

"Sheriff! Sheriff!" an excited voice cried out amid the sound of drumming hoofbeats.

A figure dressed in a tattered frock coat and a ten-gallon hat with a shapeless brim galloped toward them on the back of an undersized pinto. The face under the ill-treated hat appeared to be covered with dense brown hair streaked with gray, with only two eyes and a nose jutting from the hirsute mass. He yanked back the reins fiercely, bringing his horse to a violent halt.

"What's got you in a huff, Josh?" Krammer demanded.

"I come across a bunch of dead bodies lyin' out yonder a ways!" the shaggy-faced man replied with a mouth that contained less teeth than a chicken beak. "Somebody done kilt three fellers back there near them railroad tracks—"

"About twelve or fifteen miles from here?" Clint asked tensely, recalling what Waitley and Mike had told him about where Lloyd, Linda and Vargas had gotten off the train.

"That sounds 'bout right, young feller," Josh admitted. "I don't rightly know, 'cept it scared the bejesus outta me."

"Sheriff," Clint turned to Krammer. "I'd like to get my wagon and team settled into a livery stable. If you'll be kind enough to wait for me, I'd like to ride with you to investigate this."

"I reckon those dead men will wait for us, Clint," Krammer said. "You figure this has somethin' to do with Lloyd and the others?"

"There's only one way to find out," Clint replied.

THIRTY-FIVE

The Gunsmith and Sheriff Krammer rode along the tracks, allowing it to guide them to the location of the dead men Josh had discovered. Duke was eager to stretch his legs and Clint had to tug on the reins gently to slow the horse enough for Krammer's Morgan to keep up with them.

They soon arrived at a cluster of rock formations that surrounded the railroad—approximately fourteen miles from Yuma. Three dead men lay on the ground, their clothing splattered with blood.

"Sweet Jesus on Palm Sunday!" the sheriff rasped.

Clint brought Duke to a halt and swung down from the saddle. He approached the trio of still figures. The Gunsmith didn't recognize two of the men, but the third figure was the man who'd introduced himself as Jacob Mather in Brownsville, Texas almost two weeks before.

"You know these fellers, Clint?" Krammer asked as he dismounted.

"One of them is Jacob Manning," the Gunsmith replied. "I guess the other two are a couple of his henchmen. Hired guns for protection in Apache territory."

"Must not have been very good at their job," the lawman remarked.

"Stansfield Lloyd and Mike Vargas were better," Clint said, gazing down at the corpses.

One of the slain gunmen had been shot in the face twice, his features reduced to bloody mush. The other had been repeatedly stabbed in the chest and abdomen. Clint guessed Vargas had thrown a knife into the man and then pounced on him to finish the job. Manning's corpse was less grisly. He'd been shot through the heart.

"Why do you figure Lloyd and the Mex done this?" Krammer asked.

"The gold," Clint replied. "Manning double-crossed Mendez in Mexico in order to avoid sharing with the *bandidos* and he may have decided to cut Lloyd and Vargas out of the deal as well."

"What about the girl?"

"He might have been willing to kill her too," Clint said. "He knew she was a whore and she had a wandering eye. I doubt that he felt much loyalty or love for her."

"So they tried to get the drop on Lloyd and Vargas and lost?"

"That's *one* possibility," Clint corrected. "The other is that Lloyd, Vargas and Linda had already decided to turn against Manning before they got off the train. Lloyd and Linda seemed to be sort of close—at least Lloyd felt awfully jealous of any man who seemed to interest Linda."

"Like you?" Krammer grinned.

"What's important," Clint said, avoiding the question, "is the fact Lloyd, Linda and Vargas killed Manning and got away."

"With the gold," Krammer added.

"And my pistol," Clint stated grimly.

"Don't know that I can rightly help you, Clint," the lawman said a bit sheepishly. "You see, this is actually beyond the limits of my county so I can't very well form a posse and go after the killers. Maybe we should contact some federal marshals. . . ."

"That's all right, Sheriff," Clint assured him. "This is pretty much between Lloyd and me anyway. You could do me one big favor however."

"Can't say yes or no until I've heard what it is."

"Can you convince the liveryman to take care of my wagon and team until I get back?" the Gunsmith asked. "I'll probably be gone for a few days, but I'll pay him for his trouble when I get back."

"Well, sure," the sheriff answered, watching Clint examine the ground between the corpses and the railroad tracks. "Where will you be heading, Clint?"

"There's a set of wagon-wheel tracks here," the Gunsmith pointed at the ground. "And a set of hoofprints along side them. Seems simple enough. I've just got to follow the trail they left until it leads me to Lloyd and the others."

"They've got about half a day's head start on you, Clint," the lawman commented. "That wagon oughtta be going fairly slow, but you'll still have a hard time catching up with them."

"I've got to try, Sheriff," the Gunsmith stated as he climbed into the saddle on Duke's back. "You'll talk to that liveryman for me?"

"I said I would," Krammer nodded.

"You can also tell him if I don't return in seven days, he may as well sell my wagon and gear and make his profit that way," Clint instructed. "I won't be needing it."

THIRTY-SIX

Clint Adams wasn't a very accomplished tracker, but even he had little trouble following the trail left by the wagon and the horseman that accompanied it. Lloyd, Linda and Vargas weren't making any effort to cover their tracks, probably assuming they had plenty of time to get wherever they were going.

The trail soon led to the shore of the Colorado River which divided the Arizona Territory and the State of California. That's when he had to stop Duke and dismount to examine the ground more closely. The wagon tracks turned into the river, disappearing in the water. However, the hoofprints went in an opposite direction. His quarry had split up.

It seemed unlikely that the person on horseback had been Linda, so that meant either Lloyd or Vargas had ridden on across the Arizona prairie while the others crossed the river into California. Which trail should Clint follow?

To the Gunsmith, reclaiming his modified Colt .45 was more important than the gold shipment the outlaws had stolen south of the border. If one of the men had ridden off to get supplies or contact someone in a nearby town, either Lloyd or Vargas could be the horseman. If the outlaws had split up the gold and parted company for keeps, it seemed probable that Lloyd and Linda had ridden across the river into the next state while Vargas went his separate way.

Which man had Clint's pistol? Stansfield Lloyd was a professional gunman. At first this seemed to make him the obvious choice, but Lloyd had his Remington .44 which he'd used successfully in the past. Would he exchange his trusty weapon for the Gunsmith's Colt?

He might, yet Vargas had lost his gunbelt after Clint threw it off the train. The Gunsmith had also disposed of the cross-breed's ivory-handled dagger and hold-out knives, but Vargas had obviously had at least one more knife tucked away in his gear. If Lloyd had decided to stick with his Remington, Vargas—a knife artist who wasn't especially fond of firearms—may have taken Clint's gunbelt simply to replace his own.

Clint didn't have any trouble deciding what to do next. A wagon with two people and a chest of gold couldn't move as fast as a lone man on horseback. He'd follow the hoofprints and hope he'd catch the others later.

The sun was an orange sphere melting into the horizon when Clint trailed the horse tracks to a small town with a crudely made sign bearing the legend ARCO IRIS.

Clint's limited Spanish failed to translate Arco Iris into *rainbow,* a name that hardly suited the dreary little town. Arco Iris wasn't much larger than the Pueblo Indian hamlet El Lobo had used as a temporary headquarters.

The buildings in Arco Iris, like the Pueblo hamlet, were made of adobe. However, the style was clearly of a Spanish flavor, as if someone had transplanted a chunk of a Mexican town to Arizona. Clint entered the hamlet and cautiously glanced about the whitewashed adobe structures with their tile roofs and ornate windows. The town would have seemed deserted except for the yellow lantern light visible in a few windows and the softly played guitar music coming from a cantina.

Despite its tiny size, Arco Iris had a jailhouse with iron bars in the windows, built onto a sheriff's office. Following his habit, Clint headed for the local lawman's headquarters and dismounted. He tied Duke to the hitching-rail outside and approached the sheriff's office. The door was open.

"*Qué quiere usted*?" a voice demanded. It belonged to a fat figure seated behind a small wooden desk. His feet were propped up on the furniture, barely leaving room for a bottle of tequila.

"Sorry, friend," Clint replied. "My Spanish isn't very good."

"You a *gringo*, huh?" the fat man remarked. A sly smile crept across his bearded face. If he'd removed the tin star from his soiled shirt, he could have passed as a former member of El Lobo's gang. "Your dark skin and that sombrero fooled me for a minute. We don't get many of your kind here."

"I wouldn't guess you get many strangers of any kind," Clint commented dryly.

"Not too many," the lawman admitted as he raised the bottle to his lips. "You want somethin', *gringo*?"

"I'm looking for a man who may have entered town a few hours ago," Clint began. "My name is Clint Adams and—"

"And my name is Rameriz Santos," the sheriff shrugged. "So what?"

Clint ignored his attitude. "The man I'm looking for is a thief and a killer."

"Isn't everyone, señor?" Santos asked with a grin.

"Not quite," Clint told him. "You are the sheriff of this town, aren't you?"

"*Sí*," Santos nodded. "And the mayor and the undertaker."

"Then you should be concerned about who rides into Arco Iris."

"I care." Santos shrugged. "I don't care much for *gringos* or what they want. Nobody here does. That's why no *gringos* live here. You Anglos don't like us and we don't like you."

Clint felt his temper begin to boil, but he kept it under control. "Well, I don't intend to stay here any longer than it takes me to find the man I'm after," he explained. "The sooner I do that, the sooner I'll be on my way."

"That sounds pretty good," Santos replied. "This *hombre* you want, he's a half-breed named Vargas, no?"

Clint nodded.

"He's over in the cantina," Santos stated, lowering his feet to the floor. "We go talk to him together, okay?"

"If that's how you want it, Sheriff," the Gunsmith agreed.

Santos waddled around from behind his desk. He wore a gunbelt with a Bowie knife in a sheath positioned at a cross-draw angle on his massive belly. He couldn't have looked more like a *bandido* if he wore cartridge belts across his chest.

"I just want to make sure you ain't some *gringo* bounty hunter who thinks he can just kill a *mejicano* in cold blood," Santos stated. "And then you ride outta here and brag about how you took him in a fair gunfight."

"I'm not a bounty hunter," Clint replied. "And I'm not eager to kill anybody. Vargas either has something that belongs to me or he knows where I can find it. That's all I want from him."

"Let's go hear his side of the story," Santos said, walking toward the door.

Clint followed the sheriff outside and they headed toward the cantina across the street. His hand remained close to the pistol grips of the modified Stevens shotgun. Santos was the worst excuse for a lawman Clint had encountered for some time and he was well aware that just because a man wears a badge doesn't make him above corruption. Santos was the type who could be paid to give shelter to an outlaw like Vargas—and he might not object to shooting a *gringo* in the back if he thought he could make an additional profit in the process.

As they approached the doors of the cantina, an old man in an apron stepped outside with a broom in his hands. He saw Santos and quickly stepped aside.

"*Buenas noches, jefe,*" he said with a humble bow.

The sheriff ignored the old man, but Clint didn't fail to notice that he'd addressed Santos as *chief,* suggesting that the lawman ran his town like a bandit leader or a feudal lord. The Gunsmith despised such petty dictators. He'd pulled down more than one self-styled Nero from his throne, but he realized he couldn't play Don Quixote and pit himself against every evil-doer he encountered. As long as people are willing to knuckle under to tinhorn tyrants, there'd always be masters and slaves, one way or the other.

The inside of the cantina was shabby and drab, with half a dozen tables and twice that many chairs and a bar that consisted of a column of wooden crates with a long, wide board nailed across its top. Two coal-oil lanterns hung from ropes attached to the ceiling.

At one table sat a sad-faced man with graying hair and a withered right arm. He pressed the frets with his stony hand, the mangled fingers of the other still able to strum the cords. The music was as sorrowful as the player's appearance, yet it had a haunting, rather disturbing beauty, a melodic version of the macabre grace of a vulture in flight.

There were only three other customers in the cantina. Two younger men dressed in *peón* garb who shared a pitcher of beer seemed to concentrate on the uncanny music. The third man sat alone with a bottle of tequila, a glass and a pile of salt on a table. Mike Vargas had just poured himself a drink and was about to pinch into the salt mound when Clint and Santos entered. He didn't recognize the Gunsmith at first, but as they approached his table an expression of astonishment appeared on Vargas's face.

"This *hombre* wants to talk to you, Señor Vargas," the sheriff declared. "He thinks maybe you have something that belongs to him."

"He's loco," Vargas replied stiffly. "I never took nothin' from this *gringo*. He just wants to—"

"Stand up, Vargas," Clint snapped.

The cross-breed looked at Santos. "You gonna let him give orders in your town, Rameriz?"

"Do it, señor," the sheriff told him in a flat, hard voice.

Vargas slowly rose from his chair. He wasn't wearing a gunbelt or carrying a pistol. An ivory-handled dagger, identical to the one he'd carried on the train, was in a sheath at his hip.

"Does Lloyd have my gun?" Clint asked, his frosty gaze locked on Vargas, his hand resting on the butt on his scattergun.

"I don't know what you're talking about, *gringo*." Vargas sneered.

"You and Lloyd threw me off that train into the desert to die, Vargas," Clint stated. "You've murdered at least one innocent man and probably a lot of others I don't know about. Killing you won't bother me a bit, so you'd better talk."

"You wanta kill me, Adams?" the cross-breed smiled

as he stepped away from the table. "Then put down your guns and try to take me . . ."

He slowly drew the dagger from its sheath. The seven inch, double-edged blade reflected the lamp light like a slither of silver fire.

"*My way*!" Vargas challenged.

"That seems fair," Santos commented with a shrug. He drew his Bowie knife and offered it to Clint, handle first. "You either fight him with cold steel or you get out of Arco Iris."

Clint glanced at the Bowie knife and then glared at the smug face of Mike Vargas. The Gunsmith's expression didn't reveal the apprehension and downright fear he felt as he took the Bowie from Santos. He'd seen Vargas in action and knew the man was far better with a knife than himself. Clint had never favored bladed weapons, but he had no choice except to fight Vargas on his terms or leave without finding out any more than he knew before.

"I told you he's loco!" Vargas laughed.

Clint held the Bowie in his left hand as he backed away from Vargas and Santos. He drew the shotgun and placed it on the table occupied by the two young *peónes*. They stared up at him with surprise and awe.

"Watch my guns, *amigos*," he requested. "I don't trust your *jefe*. *Comprende*?"

"*Sí, señor*," one of the men nodded.

The Gunsmith unsheathed his Colt pistol, his eyes never leaving Vargas and Santos. He put the handgun on the table next to the Stevens. The guitar player began picking the cords in a monotonous, yet rhythmic tune that seemed to emphasize the tension of the upcoming duel.

Clint took the Bowie knife in his right hand and nodded at Vargas as he approached his opponent. The cross-breed moved to the middle of the room, his body crouched in a low fighting stance he'd known since childhood.

The guitar music ceased.

THIRTY-SEVEN

Vargas snarled and slashed out at Clint with his dagger. The Gunsmith jumped out of the path of the blade and narrowly avoided a sudden thrust as Vargas immediately altered his attack, changing tactics with swift, smooth ease.

The cross-breed swung a backhand stroke at Clint's face, missing flesh by less than an inch. The Gunsmith's leg lashed out and Vargas groaned and doubled up when Clint's boot slammed into his abdomen just above the groin. Clint moved in, trying to slash Vargas's knife arm to disable his opponent, but the cross-breed's dagger danced faster and Clint retreated.

Vargas attacked again and Clint barely dodged a dagger thrust. The Gunsmith and Vargas leaped away from each other and squared off once more. Clint raised his foot and jerked his knee forward. Vargas thought Clint was about to throw another kick and slashed low to attack the leg before he realized the tactic was a feint. Clint's left fist caught the cross-breed on the jaw and knocked him backward into a table.

Vargas whirled and lashed out at Clint, again missing the agile Gunsmith. Then he dropped into a low crouch, knife held ready, left hand poised parallel to the right. Clint adopted a similar stance, facing his deadly adversary. A sly grin slithered across Vargas's lips and Clint knew what he was about to do—at least, he *hoped* he'd guessed correctly.

The cross-breed suddenly tossed the dagger from his right hand to the left, trying to catch his opponent off guard as he had done in numerous knife fights in the past. Clint had recalled witnessing the knife duel between Vargas and one of the *peónes*. He'd expected this tactic and prepared for it. Clint struck out with the Bowie knife, the sharp edge hacking into Vargas's left hand.

Vargas screamed and staggered backward. His dagger and two severed fingers fell to the floor. He clutched his maimed hand, trying to plug up the blood that spurted from the stumps of his fingers. Clint held the Bowie high, giving the cross-breed a good look at the scarlet stain on its blade.

"Now talk!" he demanded.

"*Cristo!*" Vargas exclaimed through clenched teeth. "Stan has your gun! He's been practicing with it. Every time the train stopped he'd go do some target shooting to get used to the pistol. Said it was better and faster than his Remington."

"Did he use it to kill Manning and the other man?" Clint asked.

"*Si!*" Vargas confirmed. "He shot them down so quick they didn't have time to blink their eyes before they died."

"Why'd you two kill Manning?"

"For the gold," the cross-breed confessed. "We took most of the risks. Why should we share with him? Turned out Manning felt the same way about us. As soon as the train was out of sight, he and his men tried to gun us down. We won."

"Why'd you split up at the river?"

"Because Stan suddenly pulled a gun on me and told

me to ride on," Vargas hissed. "He said he couldn't trust me not to turn against him! *Estúpido!* Does he think he can trust that *puta* Linda? Stan tells me I don't get no gold. Says I should feel lucky 'cause he's lettin' me live and if he ever sees me again he'll kill me. So he and Linda head for California and I wind up here. . ." he squeezed his wounded hand tighter. "*Que chigada!* I hope you find him, Adams. I hope you two *bastardos* kill each other!"

"Nice seeing you again too, Vargas," Clint remarked as he backed away from his injured opponent.

When he reached the table where his shotgun and pistol lay, Clint tossed the Bowie knife to the floor and reached for his firearms. Sheriff Santos quickly waddled toward him, a smile plastered on his fat, bearded face.

"Hey, Señor Adams," he began, "what is this about gold? Maybe you could use a partner. . . ."

"Hardly," Clint replied, shoving the shotgun into its holster.

"But, señor," Santos whined, "I am not a greedy man. You could keep most of it for yourself and—"

Clint saw Vargas's right hand streak toward the back of his neck. The Gunsmith recalled the hide-out throwing knife the cross-breed had carried before and immediately realized what the man was about to do. Clint grabbed his Colt from the table, hastily aiming and cocking the pistol. He squeezed the trigger a tenth of a second too late. Vargas had already hurled his knife even as Clint fired the gun.

The thrown knife whirled across the room, turned once in midair and struck flesh. The spear-point tip plunged deeply into its victim and a cry of agony filled the cantina. The roar of Clint's Colt followed and a .45 slug smashed into Vargas's throat, tunneling through his neck to sever the spinal cord and burst vertebrae as if it were made of crystal.

Sheriff Rameriz Santos had already crashed to the floor of the cantina, the thrown knife buried in his flabby chest almost to the hilt. Clint glanced down at the trembling lump of dead blubber as he holstered the revolver.

"Looks like you folks will have to get a new sheriff," he remarked. "Try to pick a better one this time. That shouldn't be hard to do."

The joyful strumming of guitar strings suggested at least one citizen of Arco Iris fully agreed.

THIRTY-EIGHT

"So you're the Gunsmith," Sheriff Wade Ebbson remarked, gazing up at the tall, rather scruffy-looking stranger who'd just entered his office and introduced himself as Clint Adams.

"That's what some folks call me," Clint admitted.

After leaving Arco Iris, the Gunsmith had returned to the Colorado River and crossed the ford where the wagon tracks had. Locating the trail again on the opposite side of the river, he'd continued to follow the tracks into the state of California. Almost two days later, the trail led him to the town of Mortonville.

Once again, he'd headed for the sheriff's office to let the local lawman know he was in town. Sheriff Ebbson seemed to be a far better lawman than the late Ramirez Santos. Short and stocky, Ebbson looked tough enough to handle most trouble without using the .44 Colt he wore in a cross-draw holster on his belt. But he didn't seem to be an arrogant lawman, nor was he impressed by the Gunsmith's reputation—although he did seem a bit suspicious.

"What can I do for you, mister?" Ebbson inquired, obviously not convinced that his visitor was who he claimed to be.

"First of all you can call me Clint," the Gunsmith answered. Then he explained why he was in Mortonville, editing out all information that wasn't necessary to tell his tale.

"That's why you're carrying that scattergun, huh?" Ebbson frowned.

"Until I get my Colt back," Clint nodded.

"Lloyd's not wanted in this state," the sheriff began. "I don't rightly think I can arrest him for having gold he stole from the Mexican treasury anyway."

"Then he's here?" Clint asked.

The lawman shrugged. "A feller fitting his description rode into town in a wagon and he had a mighty pretty gal with him. They rode in yesterday afternoon. I don't know their names for sure, but this feller did head outside of town this morning and did some target practice with a pistol. He was close enough for us to hear him firin' his gun. The shots were fired mighty fast."

"Double action," Clint stated.

"Could be," Ebbson allowed. "Rumor I heard was they plan to catch a stagecoach tomorrow and head to San Francisco."

"Are they staying at the hotel?" Clint inquired, certain a town the size of Mortonville wouldn't have more than one.

"I've listened to your story, Clint," the sheriff began. "And I can see why you'd have a score to settle with this Lloyd feller—if that's who the man is. That still don't give you a right to blast him with that sawed-off in cold blood. Way I heard it, the Gunsmith would no more murder a feller that way than I would."

"You heard right," Clint assured him. "I plan to give Lloyd a chance to hand over what doesn't belong to him. If he refuses, I'll have to meet him in the street."

"He's been practicing with that fancy pistol," Ebbson said. "From what you've told me, he's already learned to handle it well enough to kill two men quick as a rat-tler. I don't see how you could have gotten enough time to practice with your revolver like he has and that gunbelt you're wearin' isn't a quick-draw rig."

"I'll try to avoid any shooting, Sheriff," Clint told him. "But you'd better clear the streets in case Lloyd doesn't feel the same way."

"He'll face you, Clint," the lawman frowned. "You know that."

"His decision," Clint declared.

"Yeah," Ebbson sighed. "And your funeral."

THIRTY-NINE

Sheriff Ebbson and his deputy concentrated on urging people to keep off the streets while the Gunsmith stood across from the hotel and waited. Funny things float through a man's mind when he knows he might soon be dead. Clint remembered friends and family members. The love his parents had given him as a child, the kindly advice of Bill Hickok and the day he first set eyes on Duke when the horse was just a colt—all came back to him vividly.

Your life may be over in the next few minutes, a voice seemed to tell him. *Here's what you've done with your life so far. Could you have done better? Probably. Any regrets? Naturally, but probably less than most men.* Clint had always lived by his principles so his conscience was clear. *Will you do more with your life if you get a chance after today?*

Hopefully.

Are you ready to die? That one was easy for Clint— *yes.* He had long ago accepted the fact that one day he'd die by a bullet. It was probably a better way than rotting away from old age. Clint had no fear of death itself, but he wasn't terribly eager for it to happen either.

Then he saw Sheriff Ebbson standing at one end of town and the deputy at the other. The lawmen nodded at Clint, signaling that the streets would be clear of innocent bystanders as long as necessary. Clint nodded in return. He almost reached for his pocket watch, but then remembered it was broken. Judging from the position of the sun, Clint guessed it was about two o'clock in the afternoon. Did it really matter when a man dies?

"Not as much as *how* he dies," Clint whispered as he walked across the street toward the hotel.

"Lloyd!" he shouted when he reached the middle of the street.

There was no answer, but Clint saw a curtain move at a second-story window.

"You've got something that doesn't belong to you, Lloyd," Clint called up to the window.

"Linda stays with me!" Stansfield Lloyd's gruff voice shouted from somewhere in the hotel.

"You're welcome to her," Clint assured him. "But you have a gun that belongs to me and something else that belongs to the Mexican government." Clint didn't mention that the property had been taken from the treasury. If he survived his encounter with Lloyd, he didn't want to have every greedy two-bit hootowl in the county tagging after him when he left Mortonville.

"What I have is mine, Adams!" Lloyd snarled. His wedge-shaped face appeared at the window. "I ain't givin' you nothin'!"

"Think it over, Lloyd," Clint urged. "You don't deserve another chance, but I'll give you one. Give back what you took and I'll ride on."

Lloyd laughed in reply. "You calling me out, Adams?"

"I'm giving you a choice," Clint replied simply.

Silence followed—an unnatural silence as if the entire town was holding its breath. Clint saw the curtain move again and Linda's face appeared in the window. She looked down at Clint and shook her head sadly.

An eternity of sixty seconds passed. Then Stansfield Lloyd emerged from the front door of the hotel. Dressed in black leather with his matching low-crowned hat, the sharp-faced pistolman looked like the Grim Reaper in Western garb. On the other hand, Clint was covered with trail dust and still wore his battered straw sombrero. He resembled a weary saddlebum.

Lloyd approached cautiously, his hand dangling close to the gun on his hip—the double-action Colt revolver Clint had modified years ago. The pistolman didn't wear Clint's gunbelt, of course. Lloyd was left-handed. However, the holster had been altered to fit the Colt and tied down low on Lloyd's thigh.

"Where'd you get that cannon, Adams?" Lloyd asked, referring to the sawed-off Stevens in the crude holster on the Gunsmith's belt. "If you plan on using that thing, you should have gotten it out of leather already. I bet I can empty all six rounds into you before you can draw something that heavy and clumsy."

"You probably can," Clint shrugged. "But there's been a lot of killing lately. I've lost count of the dead bodies I've seen in the last two weeks. There doesn't have to be any more."

Lloyd smiled thinly. "You must have landed on your head when we threw you off that train, Adams. You look like you're ready to ride shotgun on a Concord, but you ain't gonna take me in a gunfight. Not the way you're armed now. . . ."

"I've said my piece," Clint stated. "Guess there's nothing left to talk about."

Lloyd nodded and stepped off the plankwalk.

The pistolman strode into the middle of the street, his hard eyes locked on the Gunsmith. No one uttered a word or made a sound, yet they felt dozens of eyes follow their every move as the citizens of Mortonville watched from windows and doorways of the buildings that surrounded the two men.

Lloyd assumed the classic position, legs shoulder width apart, knees slightly bent, hand poised at the butt of the holstered Colt. His mouth pulled into an arrogant sneer as he looked at the Gunsmith's weaponry. *Jesus,* he thought with astonishment. *Adams is nuts to arm himself with a cowboy's .45 in a holster worn too high on his hip and a big, heavy sawed-off shotgun.*

However, Lloyd thought he had Clint's strategy figured out. The Gunsmith was wearing the shotgun to try to worry Lloyd. He probably planned to pretend to reach for the sawed-off and then make a fast grab for the revolver instead. Hell, a trick like that might work against a slow amateur, but it was a fool's tactic against Stansfield Lloyd. As soon as Clint made his move, Lloyd would. . .

Then he saw Clint move into a sideways stance. The Gunsmith's left side faced Lloyd, his arm held away from his body, clear of the double-muzzle of the sawed-off shotgun which protruded from the open end of the crude holster on Clint's belt. The Gunsmith's right hand slowly moved toward the pistol grip of the cut down Stevens.

Suddenly, Lloyd saw what Clint planned to do. His eyes widened with fear and his hand streaked for the Colt on his hip.

Clint's thumb cocked one of the Stevens's hammers as his hand fisted around the grip, finger finding the trigger guard. He squeezed the trigger and the shotgun bellowed. Clint felt the recoil jerk the belt at his belly. He hadn't drawn the weapon. There had been no need to. It had already been pointed at Lloyd and the buckshot pattern did the rest. All Clint had to do was cock the hammer and fire.

The blast had chopped Stansfield Lloyd's chest into a ragged, raw chunk of meat covered with shredded cloth. His corpse had been thrown seven feet by the impact of the lead pellets and he lay sprawled on his back. The modified double-action Colt had never cleared the holster.

Clint walked to the still form, ignoring the mumbled sounds of the townsfolk as they emerged from the buildings to stare at the aftermath of the gunfight. The Gunsmith knelt by the corpse and retrieved his Colt and shoved it into his belt. Then he turned and walked away from the ragged, bloodied heap that had once been Stansfield Lloyd.

FORTY

"Clint!" Linda cried as she followed the Gunsmith.

"I hear you, Linda," he assured her as he tied Duke's reins to the rear of the same buckboard Lloyd and the girl had used to ride into Mortonville.

"You've got to understand," she reached for his arm. "Stan made me do it. . . ."

"Uh-huh." Clint pulled his arm away. "Well, nobody will make you do anything now. You've lost Manning. You lost Lloyd. Now you're on your own, lady."

"What?" Linda's tone was desperate. "What the hell am I supposed to do in this crummy little town?"

"That's not my problem," he replied.

"Take me with you," she pleaded.

"Like hell," Clint muttered as he watched Sheriff Ebbson and his deputy carry the heavy steamer trunk out of the hotel.

"What are you doing with that?" Linda demanded. "That's mine!"

"The gold bars inside have *Nacional Tesorería de Mejico* stamped on them, ma'am," Ebbson told her. "Maybe you should go along with Clint to Mexico City and explain to the treasury how you've got a right to their gold."

"Mexico City?" She stared at Clint with disbelief. "You mean you're taking it back to those goddamn greasers?"

196

"It belongs to the Mexican government," Clint replied. "I'm going to take this over to Yuma, load it on my wagon and haul it south of the border to its rightful owner."

Linda looked as though an invisible hand had slapped her. "For crissake! You're serious, aren't you?"

"That's a fact," he smiled.

Ebbson and the deputy put the chest on the back of the wagon and Clint climbed into the driver's seat, taking the reins to the team.

"It was a pleasure meeting you, Clint," Ebbson grinned. "Can't say I'm all that sorry to see you go, but you sure gave this town something to talk about."

"Don't be a fool, Clint!" Linda urged. "You can have a million in gold and *me*!"

"Who wants you?" the Gunsmith replied with a shrug. "And what the hell would I do with a million in gold?"

J. R. ROBERTS

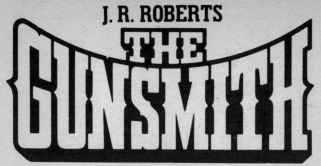

SERIES

Winners of the SPUR and WESTERN HERITAGE AWARD

Awarded annually by the Western Writers of America, the Golden Spur is the most prestigious prize a Western novel, or author, can attain.

☐ 29743-9	GOLD IN CALIFORNIA Tod Hunter Ballard	$1.95
☐ 30267-X	THE GREAT HORSE RACE Fred Grove	$2.25
☐ 47083-1	THE LAST DAYS OF WOLF GARNETT Clifton Adams	$2.25
☐ 47493-4	LAWMAN Lee Leighton	$2.25
☐ 55124-6	MY BROTHER JOHN Herbert Purdum	$2.25
☐ 82137-5	THE TRAIL TO OGALLALA Benjamin Capps	$2.25
☐ 85904-6	THE VALDEZ HORSES Lee Hoffman	$2.25